FORGIVEN

Betty Lowrey

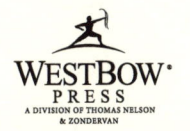

WestBow Press
A DIVISION OF THOMAS NELSON
& ZONDERVAN

Copyright © 2014 Betty Lowrey.

Cover photo by Jamie Holcomb Photography

All rights reserved. No part of this book may be used or reproduced by any means, graphic, electronic, or mechanical, including photocopying, recording, taping or by any information storage retrieval system without the written permission of the publisher except in the case of brief quotations embodied in critical articles and reviews.

WestBow Press books may be ordered through booksellers or by contacting:

WestBow Press
A Division of Thomas Nelson & Zondervan
1663 Liberty Drive
Bloomington, IN 47403
www.westbowpress.com
1 (866) 928-1240

Because of the dynamic nature of the Internet, any web addresses or links contained in this book may have changed since publication and may no longer be valid. The views expressed in this work are solely those of the author and do not necessarily reflect the views of the publisher, and the publisher hereby disclaims any responsibility for them.

Any people depicted in stock imagery provided by Thinkstock are models, and such images are being used for illustrative purposes only. Certain stock imagery © Thinkstock.

ISBN: 978-1-4908-4959-1 (sc)
ISBN: 978-1-4908-4960-7 (hc)
ISBN: 978-1-4908-4958-4 (e)

Library of Congress Control Number: 2014915534

Printed in the United States of America.

WestBow Press rev. date: 09/24/2014

LIST OF CHARACTER

GARCIA FRENCH, HAS BEEN HIRED by a nameless man, 'the boss' to kidnap a small child. For two thousand dollars, French is willing to face Capital Punishment. Unthinking, French bumbles the first try, succeeds in the last. No matter how innocent Garcia seems or incapable of doing the job, kidnapping is a serious matter, an evil deed, justified by death or life in prison, if he is caught.

Onie Smutts, is the girlfriend of Garcia French, with a twisted mind and body aged by drugs, Onie's past weighs heavily on her mind, particularly the fact she gave away her children. When her boyfriend brings the little girl to her home for safe keeping until the 'moneydrop', Onie seems to believe the baby she gave up for adoption has come home.

Beatrice Shaw, 'Bitty', beloved care-taker of three year old Ruthie has moved with the family to a new city due to the fact she has no one else. A widow, Beatrice on occasion talks to her dead husband, Larry, as she 'works through problems.' Loyalty to Ruthie and Ellen has become a labor of love. Beatrice scripture is, "We are perplexed, but not pressed down."

Ellen E. Anderson, the one whose life we share allows us to decide if it is by a twist of fate things happen to people in life or whether faith plays a huge role in the eyes of a believer. Divorced from Jeffrey she struggles financially while building a network of women who stand with her. They are aware of Ellen's faith and unfaltering intention to raise her child in the knowledge of the Lord. Ellen's scripture is, "As for me and my house we will love the Lord."

Ruthie, born to Jeffrey and Ellen Anderson, named Ruth Elizabeth Anderson, is a child with such joy in her heart you want to participate. Capricious, fun and loving, Ruthie relies on Ellen and Bitty, giving them something to think about on a daily basis. She wins the heart of the neighbor who has forbidden her setting foot on the property next door. Beloved of Bitty, Ruthie is kidnapped, drugged and found in the arms of another woman. Her scripture; Trust in the Lord with all your heart and lean not to your own understanding. "What's understanding?" She asks.

Anne Graves, Ellen's friend who is also divorced and has a son, knows Ellen through the Nursing Program. Divorced from Andrew, Anne's livelihood is precarious due to finances, weather and circumstance. When the weeks of ice and snow make traveling the roads hazardous, Anne accepts an invitation to spend nights in Ellen's home. She becomes intrigued by Ellen's faith which is foreign to her own background. Her scripture is, "I was a stranger and you took me in."

Harriet Becker, wants nothing to do with anyone and trusts no one. When the ice storm comes, and the furnace quits she prevails on the ladies next door, arriving with an attitude, to leave as a gracious friend due to Ruthie's tenacity in winning her over. Through the ordeal, the others realize Harriet was once a woman of substance who became a recluse God was willing to change. Harriet's scripture has to be found. Again.

Daniel Gates has come to Middlebury for the opening of Hutson's. There will be many social events and he is a bachelor needing an escort. Due to the weather, lacking adequate footwear he meets Ellen working in an old friend's shoe store and is immediately smitten. In a matter of days he watches as her life spirals out of control and he is drawn into the trauma of her child's kidnapping. Daniel's scripture will become Ellen's scripture. "Entreat me not to leave thee, or to return from following after thee, for whether thou goest, I will go."

James and Salena E. Lewis, Ellen's parents, have been separated from their daughter, a matter of personal issues having to do with Ellen's philandering husband. The last to believe, Ellen remained loyal to her husband and has not mended the broken relationship. The parents are candidates to be tapped for ransom, coming to Ellen; they ask forgiveness. Their scripture deals with emotionally hard times. "He will not leave you comfortless."

Captain Chester Mayfield, the backbone of the investigation, is reluctant to turn matters of the city over to the Federal Bureau of Investigation, whether by a twist of fate or faith, when he unknowingly finds Ruthie, he realizes his life has also changed. Chester tires of living alone. His scripture is Ecclesiastes 9:4 Anyone who is among the living has hope.

Andrew Graves and son, Andy, are evident characters in the background; of course Andy is an innocent child, but his father is self-centered, criticizing Anne on a regular basis and always looking for something to assuage his needs, but Andrew's story remains to be told.

Dedication

For Bob, strong, resilient and lasting. Thank you for loving me.

Thank you to Debbie and Kerri for computer expertise.
Special thank you to Tori for providing Ellen's beautiful image
To Jamie Holcomb Photography and to our Heavenly Father for
the inspiration and to understand He loves us problems and all.

Beginning Quote

He that cannot forgive others breaks the bridge over which he must pass himself, for every man has need to be forgiven.
Thomas Fuller 1608

CHAPTER 1

"Few days' surveillance," Garcia French finished telling Onie his plans for the job he'd been given, "then bam, grab the kid, deliver her, and take the money." He stretched out on the sofa, grinned up at Onie. "Piece of cake."

"It's a shame." Onie shook her head, sadly remembering her own days when she was raising children. "Mine were taken away from me. You think that's the reason someone is taking that little girl from her mommy?"

"Whatta I know?" Garcia replied. "All I know is, the man said take the girl, one way or another. Get the woman first, if I have to, and she'll bring the little one to me."

"How do you think it feels, losing your kid?"

"I don't know; how does it? I heard you took your kids down to family services."

Onie shrugged. "I didn't think you knew that." She sighed. "It still hurts."

"Didn't know you then," Garcia replied. "Heard the story, though."

"Well, I had no help. Got tired of doin' it all by myself."

"Shouldn'ta had kids in the first place."

"Had them before I knew what was happening; time I figured it out, had two."

"Thought it was three." Garcia raised up from the ratty old sofa, staring at Onie until she squirmed, uncomfortably, and turned away.

"That one don't count. He was adopted into a good family." She sighed. "A little boy." Remembering brought sorrow. "Wished I'd kept that one."

"You weren't cut out to be a mother."

"What do you know about it?"

"Look at you, smoking like a chimney, and you like your habit too much when you know we can't afford it."

"I'm nervous," Onie complained. "It calms me."

"No, it makes you high, puts you on a cloud; you don't know whether you're comin' or goin'." Garcia gave a graveled laugh. "Probably what's wrong with that one I'm relievin' of her kid."

"What's made you so mean today?" Onie gave him the look.

"Don't look at me that way, Onie. I'm the one gotta job. You ain't."

"I'm the one got a warm house," Onie replied. "So don't go gettin' all uppity at me, Garcia French." She leaned over him, her eyes squinted angrily. "You ain't fed my habit in days, and I'm about to go out of my mind. Maybe I'll kick you out and take in someone else."

Raising up, Garcia swung his feet off the couch to the floor. "You would, wouldn't you?"

"You bet your mother's Bible, I would."

"I don't ever recollect my mother having a Bible. You neither." He knew he better console Onie. "Just let me get the kid and collect the dough, and we're all set."

"You better treat me right, Garcia," she threatened. "I could let the word out."

Garcia's eyed Onie sternly. "You do, it won't be me comin' after you." His lips tightened, "Grapevine says the boss don't mind losin' them that cause him trouble."

ELLIE PULLED THE SHEET SNUGLY around Ruthie's small body, kissed her daughter on the cheek, and then stepped back to study the tiny replica of her. Everyone said Ruthie looked just like her. But … who they were on the inside was different. Maybe because Ruthie had another person's blood running through her veins. Ellie sighed, thinking, *Mom's and Dad's, and Jeffrey's, and all those who had been before either of them.*

Bitty would be here soon, and she would have to hurry. Tossing the mane of dark hair on top of her head, she pushed a clasp through the center; tried to settle the curls into some array of order so Mrs. McCallister wouldn't be after her; dabbed on a touch of Éclair, the lipstick company's description that fell somewhere between rust and mocha; and hurried down the stairs just as Bitty came huffing through the door.

"Ruthie still asleep?" Bitty backed out of the way. Ellie hoisted a bag full of books onto one shoulder and struggled to fit a hobo bag and her lunch into the other arm as she reached for a light jacket on the inside door knob.

"She's asleep." Ellie dug into the hobo, bringing a chain of keys to the surface. Poking one finger through the chain, she pushed through the door, suddenly remembering the light bill was due. "Bitty, could you fill out the check I've signed, on the kitchen counter, put it into the envelope, and see that it gets into the mail? Today! Or they will be cutting our lights. You know I've already gone through that with the gas company."

"Sure." Bitty patted a fleeing arm, closed the door, and went into the kitchen. The check was on the counter, with Saturday's date. Ellie had good intentions, but with her schedule, it was a wonder she accomplished as much as she did. Nursing school, part-time job at the shoe store, and most weekends at the hospital, enough, Bitty thought, to break the proverbial camel's back! If Jeffrey didn't take Ruthie on weekends, she would.

That's where she came in, wasn't it? Three years ago, she had lived in a different town, and so had Ellie. Jeffrey had hired her to do general cleaning on houses after his men finished their jobs, and the houses were ready for the new owners. Then there had been the slack time, when he sent her to his and Ellie's. "She keeps the books," he explained, "and things got a bit hectic, so I promised if she'd keep everything up-to-date for me, I'd help her catch up on the home needs." That's where Bitty really came in.

Those last two years, not only had Bitty cleaned new houses in preparation for Jeffrey's new owners, but any spare time she helped Ellie. "What would I do without you?" Ellie was one to hug her generously, plant a kiss on Bitty's forehead, forever grateful. Jeff, on the other hand, felt as long as a person was paid, that was it, nothing more expected, nothing else forthcoming. Do the job and leave. Show up next time.

Sighing, Bitty filled in the amount, inserted both the check and billing stub in the envelope, and started to rise. Beneath the light bill was a check with her own name, Beatrice Shaw, signed by Ellen. Funny that she could have forgotten Friday was payday. Ruthie and Ellen had become so much a part of her own, and Bitty didn't charge family. "You have to be paid, in full, Beatrice," Ellen had scolded. "You have needs, and your husband's pension won't cover everything."

"Let's make a deal. You don't call me Beatrice, and I will take pay."

"Deal." Ellen had smiled, placed the seal of kiss on Bitty's forehead, and promised. "I don't know why you don't like your name. It is a nice name."

"My parents thought so," she replied, "but my brother couldn't say Beatrice, and they all called me Bitty."

"How many brothers?" Ellen loved to hear about Bitty's life.

"Two."

"Tell me about Lawrence, your husband."

"Lawrence called me *Bitty* or *itty bitty*," Bitty laughed. "You know the story."

"Married fifteen years, Lawrence was a truck driver. You rode the states with him, helped drive." Ellen would sigh at that point in the telling. "How in the world did your feet reach the gas pedal?" She would study Bitty, appreciatively, "and then, Lawrence got sick."

"In the beginning, we tried to go on as usual. We would take the routes we knew I could drive, mostly interstate, just to help when he wasn't feeling really well. Then, even though it was five years in the making, we realized it was time to give up the truck. Larry couldn't climb the steps too well, and it was creating arthritis in me," Bitty's voice would wander away, reliving those days. "So I went to work at the newspaper, wrapping papers, had my own car route, and was able to check on Larry when I needed."

"I wish I had known you then, Bitty." Ellen's voice was gentle and kind. "I could have helped you. I could have been your friend."

"There was no help. It was incurable." Bitty smiled through tears. "You're my friend now. Sometimes I think that is more important at this time of my life, even than it was then. I had my brothers. But they had their families. It was kind of sad, like Larry's dying left me with no one."

"Then," Ellen would say in an important voice. "Along came Ellen E. Anderson." They would smile at each other. "By way of Jeffrey G. Anderson." Ellen always knew when times were getting tough, or moments sad, for Bitty. Now there was only Ellen, Ruthie, and Bitty. Jeffrey George Anderson was living in their former hometown with his girlfriend. During the year there Jeff and Ellen's home had been blessed by the cutest and smartest little brown-eyed, dark-haired baby girl Bitty had ever seen. Jeffrey, on the other hand, was too busy to notice.

Blessed. That was the word Ellen used. Bitty wasn't too sure what the definition of blessed meant. Ellen said, "Ruthie came from God's love, Bitty. No one can tell me any different. Jeff and I are blessed."

Bitty was glad Ellen felt blessed by God, because Jeffrey was bowing out, even then. She was first aware of it when she would leave her home early mornings to clean the new houses Jeffrey was building across town. She wondered why his truck would be parked at the house on Rhone Drive that early. His men didn't arrive for work until eight.

Then one day she asked Ellen.

"He's working, going to sites, making notes of what his men will need that day."

In the beginning, she believed Ellen's explanation ... until she heard a couple of Jeff's workers in another room.

"How long until the wife finds out about this one?"

Not meaning to eaves drop Bitty had straightened to listen, letting the broom stand still for a moment.

"She never knew about the others either, is my guess," the second man replied. From that moment on, Bitty found herself on guard, watchful for Ellen, whom she had come to love as the daughter she never had.

Ellen was still attending church services, wrapped up in loving little Ruthie. Faithful in all things, Ellen appreciated the times when Bitty was allowed to help out. "I manage to keep all the bills paid," she would say, "but sometimes I get behind in the posting. And this house!" She would sigh, stoop over Ruthie's bed, kiss her daughter on the forehead, and then head for the home office. "Thanks, Bitty. I don't know what we would do without you."

"Did you go to church Sunday?" Asking, Bitty could gauge the atmosphere.

"Yes, just Ruthie and me. Jeff was working." Pausing with one hand on the office door, she would give Bitty that direct soul-searching stare. "Did you?"

That was before it all broke loose, and they moved to a new city. They didn't talk about church attendance as much these days, since sometimes Ellen had to work on Sunday. *Besides,* Bitty thought, *she might not know how to act in church herself.* People come from different walks of life. She knew about church, but as Ellen said, she had not given herself completely to it.

Now Bitty placed the light bill inside the small metal box on the outside wall of the house. She and Larry hadn't attended church, though as he lay dying, they'd spoken of it. "Maybe we should have gone," he'd said to her. "We still believe there's a God."

Bitty wondered, was there really more to it than that? Where was God when Larry became ill and still a young man? What was God thinking now, about little Ruthie asleep upstairs in the bed, her momma having to work to make ends meet because her daddy didn't care and thought child support was a waste of money. His. Ellen was trying to make her way through nursing school to find a better way of life to care for Ruthie.

"Besides," Ellen would say, "I think serving others is an honorable position, Bitty. When I was little, I played nurse, a lot. But back then I didn't know it cost money to be a nurse. Even with the grants, there's a lot we have to do without."

What business did Beatrice Shaw have taking care of an infant? She guessed if it was serving someone's needs, she'd rather be helping Ellen and Ruthie than anyone else she knew. "Brrr," she shuddered. "It's a good thing Ellen got her sweater. If this weather don't warm up soon, we won't get our tulips planted in the back yard like I promised Ruthie." Anyway, Ruthie would be three soon. A lot of water ran under the bridge in three years' time. If Bitty loved anyone, she guessed it was Ruthie, the most.

"Tests today!" The blackboard message blared in their faces as each student filed into Room 104. Fourth floor was in turmoil.

"I can't remember the definition, let alone give an oral account," a familiar voice chortled. "Were we given this material to study? I don't see it on my study sheet."

"Check your notes thoroughly." Mrs. McCallister's voice, cultured and cool, came through the door. As an instructor, she was allowed to wear street clothes. Today Eva McCallister was dressed in a two-piece power suit in royal blue, her upswept hair looked as though she had just had it done, and her nails were immaculate as well.

"What's going on with you?" Merelee Fith called from the back. A swish of white leg passed by Ellen's seat as Merelee advanced from the rear and stood before Mrs. McCallister, examining their instructor. Waving one finger mid-air, Merelee tipped her head to one side and continued staring. "What? No baggy sweater, no over-stacked book bag, no lunch tied up neatly in a hankie and crammed between your notebooks, such as we lowly students have to wear?"

Everyone in the class room laughed. Only Merelee could pull off those questions. The rest sat quietly, waiting, while Mrs. McCallister erased the test warning off the blackboard. "We are going to begin in five minutes. If you have questions, you may confer with each other. Today there will be no open books, nor discussions, once we begin."

Merelee sauntered back to her desk. "Me thinks the lady has a date." She sank into her chair. "Good Lord, you don't think she's going to keep us in here all day, do you?"

The instructor paused, momentarily, beside Ellen's chair. "You asked me to let you know if there would be any change of schedule, but I think you have already become aware of clinical, beginning next week."

"Yes, ma'am." Ellen nodded. "I have someone that can arrive early to stay with my little girl."

Ellen closed her eyes so tight she thought she could pull up the written words from the pages she had studied. It was there, she knew it was there, but where? There were always questions asked in such a way one had to study them over and over, knowing full well that one question answered wrong could mean the difference in passing or failing. One instructor taught differently from the rest. It had taken the first three tests for all of the students to realize Mrs. Grandin, another instructor, thought in an unusual way. Often test material would include subjects they had never discussed in open class. Merelee always complained, saying it wasn't fair, but was it not? Ellen realized if they were going to make it, they had to read every word. "That's why we have books," her mind whispered, but Mrs. McAllister cared whether they passed or failed.

Glancing warily across the aisle, she saw Anne struggling too. Anne, with skin as white as alabaster, gray eyes, and long dark lashes, had become Ellen's true friend. And as life would have it, Anne was going through a bad time too. Neither she nor Ellen had planned a failed marriage, but it had happened. Anne's husband was paid a five-figure salary every month, not bad for the area they came from, but he shared not one cent with Anne. When he agreed to keep Andy, their son who was two, it was only on condition the child support would stop. Anne was on her own. Andrew would keep Andy through the week. Anne could have him on weekends. But where?

Anne's mother was an alcoholic, abusive and critical of her only daughter. The weekends were a mess when Anne and Andy came to stay. Anne's stepfather had moved out long ago. Knowing Anne from age two, perhaps he felt she was his own and offered a place for Anne and Andy when his former wife became unbearable. Anne confided there really was no place they found peace. Andy was growing, faster every day, it seemed. She had to get life right. She needed three years, at least, to become a registered nurse. Nursing school was hard. It required concentration. With everything else in turmoil, how could she go on? Now, before the instructor said the test time had begun, Anne was trying to remember what she had studied.

The words jumbled across her mind, nothing solid, nothing with meaning. She felt the tears well up in her eyes and slide down her cheeks. Then, just briefly, a hand reached across the aisle, took hers, and squeezed. Faintly she heard words of encouragement.

"It will be all right, Anne. This is not Mrs. Grandin." Her heart eased, thumping more quietly inside her chest, as Mrs. McCallister said, "Now we shall begin."

When the test ended, from the back Merelee asked, "Did you peeps ace it?"

"What a day!" Anne searched through her purse for the cell phone she had turned off before class. "I don't know if I made a good enough grade, Ellen."

"Casting bread before the water, we shall wait and see," Ellen quipped. "Are you headed home or staying the night?"

Anne's lip trembled just a second before she replied. "I don't have enough gas to go home." She twisted the handle of her book bag. "Which means I don't have money for a room."

"Can you make it to my house?" Ellen's eyes filled with concern. "Do you want to leave your car here?" Reaching out, she pulled Anne to her side. "Come on, Duckie. You can stay with Ellen E. Anderson tonight."

"Are you sure?" Something between a sob and relief sounded in her voice.

"Just you, me, and Ruthie, Duckie, and Bitty, if she wants to stay. I bet Bitty has made a pot of soup that will make your taste buds melt."

Anne knew about Bitty. If Ellen weren't such a good friend, she would feel jealous. "If you're really all right with me coming?" Ellen was already pulling her down the hall, through the doors to the parking lot, and outside, unlocking the door to a small black car. "I'll get my things," she said, heading toward her old car. From the trunk she drew out a small overnight bag.

They passed the dorms and the rental houses filled with those able to pay a term's rent. "I looked into one of those," Anne said quietly. "The worst requirement was money."

"Yeah." Ellen grinned. "Kind of gets you right here, doesn't it?" She smacked her chest. "Here I am trying to make it on a widows' penance, with a hungry child."

"Widow?" Anne's eyebrows rose. "Last I heard Mr. Anderson was alive and well."

"Same thing." Ellen smirked. "He is gone from my life."

"I don't see how you can smile. I know you hurt inside just as much as I do."

"But," Ellen's head tilted sideways, staring into Anne's solemn eyes. "Does it help?"

"What is it with you," Anne stared back, "and all this *bread cast on the water* stuff?"

Ellen chuckled. "Cast your bread upon the waters is a Bible verse, meaning if you care about someone else, it will come back to you. You know, similar to the verse where Jesus explained if we give a cup of water to someone in need, we will be blessed." She grinned foolishly, "I guess I'm being selfish, taking you home with me. I want to be blessed."

"You are one strange girl."

"I've heard that before." Ellen grimaced.

"In a good way," Anne replied, smiling.

Bitty watched, in the following days. Sometimes Anne rode home with Ellen. Other times, she heard the battered old Chevrolet stop in front and knew Anne needed a place to stay again. Like the proverbial woman in the Bible that Ellen had made her aware of, Bitty cooked stew, or soup, or chili, making the ingredients stretch farther and farther. As the woman in the Bible, she guessed, caring for her own.

"Stars in your crown," Ellen would tease. Ruthie loved Anne, always happy to give up her bed and climb in bed with her mother.

Bitty loved them all. Sometimes talking out loud, she would tell Larry, "This is the family we were meant to have." Shaking her head, she would look to heaven and ask, "Why did you have to die too soon?"

Thanksgiving arrived, uneventful except for Ellen working at the shoe store and Bitty taking Ruthie home with her.

She noticed Jeffrey hadn't used the opportunity that was his, to have his daughter on the holiday. Ellen didn't mention it, and neither did she.

Fall turned into winter. Winter brought blasts of air that rattled down the chimney of the old house, while Bitty made sleeves out of old sheets, filled them with sand from Ruthie's sandbox, and placed them beneath each door.

"I think you better make some more of those snakes and put them on the windows," Ruthie announced, stooping to blow onto the glass pane and watch her breath turn to frost. "And they would look prettier if they were colorful, and we sewed eyes on them."

Ellen came home to find the windows decorated. "Isn't that my old skirt I threw in the rag bag?"

"It was your skirt," Bitty agreed.

"Now it's one of our snakes," Ruthie exclaimed. "Aren't they pretty?"

"You bet your buttons, Sweetums." Ellen smiled, picking Ruthie up from the floor, hugging her tightly to her chest. "I love those eyes."

"Those are Bitty's buttons," Ruthie said, solemnly. "From her jar of buttons."

"How are you doing in class?" Bitty slipped one arm into the heavy wool coat, and then the other, wrapping the attached scarf around her neck. She had seen the stack of papers on Ellen's dining room table. Spread out and quite visible, the evolving grades seemed to be suffering from those in the beginning of the year.

Ellen shrugged, arching her shoulders to relieve tiredness. "It is getting pretty hard, and now I'll have more hours at the shoe store since Christmas is just around the corner. I'm going to have to burn the midnight oil." She turned worried eyes from Ruthie to Bitty. "Will you be able to stay with Ruthie when I work late, maybe stay over on those nights?"

"You can sleep in my bed, Bitty." Ruthie clasped her arms around Bitty's knees. "Or I can sleep with you, if you are afraid."

Bitty patted Ruthie's hair. She loved that child like she was her own. "We'll work something out." She stooped, placed a kiss on Ruthie's head, and turned to the door.

"I saw those tears, Bitty," Ellen whispered. "She has that power, doesn't she?" Quick as a whip, Ellen pressed Bitty to her side. "You are one grand dame, Itty-Bitty."

CHAPTER 2

"It's almost Christmas, Bitty." Ruthie was whispering so low, Bitty could hardly hear. "I collect all the money I find on the floor, by the washer, just anywhere I can find it." She stared up into Bitty's face, her eyes as wide as saucers. "I asked Mommy was it stealing if I find money in the house and keep it. She said no because that would be like finding a hen with a tooth." Ruthie giggled. "Do hens really have teeth?"

"Not that I know about," Bitty replied. "And what will you do with this money?"

"I'll buy gifts."

Bitty found herself laughing, and Ruthie laughed too. It was their secret joke. A game had begun with all three participating.

"Found any hen's teeth, lately?" Ellen asked one evening.

"Not a one," Bitty replied. "But I keep looking."

Ruthie wondered why they laughed, if they hadn't found anything.

Ellen's schedule for work increased right along with the nursing school's. Anne came now and then, bringing gifts of peanut butter, eggs, and cheese. Ruthie watched, waiting until Bitty arrived the next morning to ask, "Bitty, how do you think Anne gets that cheese? Do you think she is robbing a store?"

Bitty sat down by the small wall shelf that acted as a bar for Ruthie's morning snacks. Lifting the apron skirt to her face, she laughed softly behind its material before looking into Ruthie's worried eyes. "I think Anne has had such a rough time, someone somewhere has given her those items, and Anne wants to share them with you and Momma because when she needs to, Momma lets her stay here."

A much relieved Ruthie eased through the morning, her little voice carrying up and down the stairs of the old house as she sang, "He's got the whole world in His hands." Dusting and sweeping, Bitty joined right in. *Larry,* she said, quietly and silently, only to him and the Maker above, *I didn't know much about God's love, and I was really mad when you died, but this little girl is teaching me happiness in a fine new way. Maybe one of these days I'll understand a little more what it is all about.*

Ruthie lay listening to the familiar drone of the old house. In the next room, the drip of water from the faucet plop, plop, plopped. Then there was the whirr of the ceiling fan in Mommy's room. The sun was already up, and it was later than she meant for it to be. Last night she told Mommy she would say good-bye this morning and good luck with the test. Because Mommy kept saying *shush,* she knew Mommy was studying for a test. Now it was too late to say bye or have a good test.

What if she were alone? She listened. Right then, she heard the screen door shut. Someone's footsteps sounded on the wood porch floor. *Be careful. There's a hole just before you go down the steps.* When Mommy bought the house, the porch was painted bright red, and Mommy said it looked good. Then, after everything was all moved in, except the refrigerator that wouldn't go through the door, the moving man turned the refrigerator up on one side. That's when the corner of the refrigerator went through the floor, and Mommy said, "Well, I guess it wasn't as good as I thought."

"What can you expect from a ninety-five-year-old house?" That's what they kept saying that day as they put away clothes, ran up and down the stairs, and got tired.

"I have an aunt," Ellen would explain sometimes. "She is ninety. She has a lot of aches and pains. But she also has a lot of character."

That day Mommy looked at Ruthie and said, "I think our house has a lot of character, don't you, Sweetums?"

Sweetums. Ruthie thought about her nickname. Sweetums was just one of them. She liked when Mommy called her Sweetums and talked to her in a way that she knew was strictly between the two of them. "What is strickly?" She asked once when Mommy said, "This is strictly between you and me, Sweetums." She forgot what was strictly between them, but Mommy said the word meant exactly, faithfully, true, between me and you. She had to count on that a lot, since Daddy wasn't with them anymore. And she counted on Bitty, too.

Ruthie slid feet-first from the bed. The floor creaked and settled. She slipped her feet into the rabbit fur house shoes Bitty brought last week and started down the stairs. From the landing, to the second turn that led to the first floor, she could walk now without holding on to the banister, but Bitty said, "Hold on. Hold on. No need to fall."

She tip-toed around the coat wall, peeped into the kitchen, and saw Bitty standing in front of the sink washing dishes. With a rush, she ran and threw her arms around Bitty's legs

"Got you." She knew Bitty would act scared to death, and then she would turn and hug her to her body.

"Awww," Bitty cried out. "Mercy. Mercy. Who has got hold on me?" Bitty's arms were already around Ruthie, hugging and laughing. "Sleepy head. I thought you were never going to wake up."

"I wanted to, but I just didn't."

"What do you want for breakfast?"

"Froot Loops." Ruthie crawled up onto the stool. The shelf on the wall was just wide enough to hold three plates, and just deep enough for a glass to sit in front, but there were only two stools. When Bitty ate with them, they sat at the table. "Yellow." Bitty was holding the cabinet door open, waiting for Ruthie to tell her which bowl. "Can we plant tulips today?"

"Not today. It's too cold. But you can help me roll papers."

"That's not much fun."

"Then I'll roll papers and you can watch Dora. How does that sound?"

They settled into their usual morning's rhythm. It was three o'clock. Bitty had rolled all the papers and was taking them out to her old car. She would never have been able to take care of Ruthie if Joe hadn't told his friend about Bitty.

"I told him you worked here at the newspaper office for ten years, and I never worried once that you wouldn't get your route finished, no matter what the weather," Joe used to tell her. "I told him, if you want someone you can trust, then she's the girl for you."

That was how she met Jeffrey Anderson. He had come into the newspaper office to run an advertisement. When he inquired if Joe knew any reliable people, Bitty was the one. A lot of history lay between her and Joe. Eventually Bitty's life became involved with the Anderson household. Then came the divorce and Bitty's heart all tangled up with the baby girl. When she told Joe, he said, "Bitty, if you are set on moving to that town and need employment other than keeping that little girl, you go see Jack. It's the same wherever we go. People need people they can count on. I got a feeling that girl's going to need you too."

That was exactly what she did. With Larry's pension and rolling advertisements for the weekly throw out, in a new town she could make it. She knew a thing or two about cash registers and 7-Elevens, but it was the hours got her. She'd rather sleep nights and work days. Too many times reliable people wouldn't take the night shift. Sometimes night shift was left to the teenagers that quit their last year of school. For Bitty, one job always led to another. If she was dependable in one, she had no problem finding others. She thought maybe the other jobs found her. "You want a house sitter you can trust, call Beatrice Shaw." That's what a lot of people said. "She'll keep your kids from killing each other. She'll feed your dog or cat. Just don't call on her through the week."

One hundred dollars a weekend was pretty good money. All she had to do for houses was stay there. They left food, clean sheets on the bed, and rented movies for her. Now the kids were a different matter. That paid more. Under age sixteen, she said forget it. Over sixteen, she wasn't really responsible for them, just a guarantee to the parents there would be no parties, and the kid had to be accountable to someone, didn't they? Besides, she had Ruthie. She liked other little kids, but Ruthie was special. Ruthie needed her.

Bitty had to smile. She had met some pretty good kids in this town. Seemed like college towns had lots of parents who were teachers, and they had no family with which to leave their kids or know the house would be all right until they returned home. Some of the kids were fun. When all else was said and done, it was a way of having kids, wasn't it?

Back inside, shutting the door again, Bitty laughed out loud remembering the Hatcher kid.

"What's funny?" Ruthie turned to stare, leaving the television's screen for a moment while Dora struggled up a mountain. She liked the sound of Bitty's laughter. It was kind of like a swish and the way she sounded when she had a cold, dry and husky.

"I was thinking of that Hatcher kid. Do you remember? I told you he wanted me to teach him how to dance before he picked up his girl for the dance?"

"Show me." Ruthie hopped down from the sofa to stand in front of Bitty.

Bitty held out one arm, placed the other on Ruthie's shoulder. "Now, like I said before, we will walk two steps forward and then back one.

"You are too tall, Bitty."

"You think I'm tall?" Bitty gave a chortled laugh, remembering the Hatcher kid. "Billy was six feet tall. Now that is over a foot taller than me. And feet … I can't tell you how long that boy's feet were … just when they stepped on mine … well, mine were covered up."

"I can't dance, Bitty. I'm too little." Ruthie plopped back onto the sofa. "Did you like him? That Billy boy?"

"You bet. He was a good kid."

Ruthie considered the information. "Did you like him better than me?"

"Let me think." Bitty placed one finger to her cheek, as a serious expression dawned in her eyes. Then she squinted and made a humming noise. "No. But I liked him."

"Daddy doesn't like me."

Bitty's head jerked around to face Ruthie, a solemn look covering her whole face now. "What makes you think that?" She sat down and placed one hand on Ruthie's pants leg.

"He doesn't come to see me, and he doesn't call me on the phone."

"Maybe he is busy."

"No. He has lots of time," Ruthie sighed as she snuggled closer to Bitty's side.

"Don't you remember? From the time the big yellow bus ran in the afternoon, he was home and he'd watch ballgames while Mommy worked on the books, and I'd sit by him." She leaned forward and stared straight into Bitty's face. "If I was watching Dora, Daddy would say, 'All right, little girl, you've had enough. It's my time.'"

Surprise shone in Bitty's eyes. "You can't remember that. You were too little."

"I asked Mommy if that was real, or did I dream it. She said it was real. Daddy liked ballgames." Ruthie sighed. "I was two. Now I'm almost four."

"Honey, you are three."

"I feel four."

"I declare, sometimes I think you are older than me. How did you get this way?"

"It's div-orse." Bitty pressed the strands of Ruthie's hair down on her head where electricity from the sofa material made them stand up and wave in the air.

"You mean *divorce*."

"Whatever it is that takes little girls away from daddies and mommas."

"But you love being with Mommy."

"I have to be," Ruthie sighed, matter of fact. "She said she would die without me." For a second she seemed to be thinking on an inside matter. "I don't think Daddy even knows we're gone." She clutched Bitty's hand. "I didn't care if Daddy turned Dora off; I just liked to sit by him."

Searching in her own mind, Bitty thought to put happy times in the child's mind. "You know what I think? I think it is time for us to hit the road and throw out papers." She bent to straighten Ruthie's socks. "Now get your shoes on, and maybe we will stop at the shoe store on the way back and see your mommy a minute."

Bitty examined the wall clock. By four in the evening, Ellie would be changing clothes to go to work up town. By eight o'clock, she would be home with Ruthie, unless Schumacher needed her to stay longer.

"Let's see, now. Have we learned anything today?" Finger and thumb to the bridge of her nose, Bitty thought. "Mercy, I am falling down on my job. When your momma wanted me to stay with you, I said, what am I to do with a little girl? She said, love her and teach her something new every day."

"You taught me how to count to ten."

"Mostly your momma did that." Chagrined, Bitty knew she had failed again.

"You said people shouldn't take wooden nickels, and you said that meant things that aren't real." Perplexed, Ruthie tried to think of other things Bitty had taught her. "I can't tie my shoestrings yet, but I am still trying."

"Yes. You are."

"I know the Lord's Prayer."

"We had to learn that together."

"I believe it."

"I'm glad you do."

"We need to work on that Sam twenty-three, Bitty."

"*Psalms* 23."

"Haven't you ever walked alone, Bitty?" Ruthie stood up, peering intently into Bitty's eyes. "Me and Momma are having to walk alone, 'cept she says God is walking right there by us, and we can't even see Him." Ruthie sliced the air with her arms. "Can you feel Him, Bitty?"

"Lord, no, I can't feel Him, child."

"Are you praying, Bitty? 'Cause, Momma says we don't call on God in vain. What does vain mean again, Bitty. I forgot."

"You're smarter than me, child. Maybe I was prayin'. Vain? Now let me think. I believe it means if you don't need Him, then don't call right now. How does that sound?"

"I guess it's all right. See, Bitty, you taught me something today. I won't bother God until I really need Him. After all, if He's right here by my side and I can't see Him, everything is all right too, ist it?"

"*Isn't* it," Bitty corrected. "Now, let's get our jackets and scoot out of here."

CHAPTER 3

They made it through the year. Ellen was ready to receive her licensed practical nurse certificate. Bitty and Ruthie arrived for the ceremony early enough to sit in chairs near the front and see Ellen received the piece of paper she had worked hard to attain. Bitty had thought to buy a long-stemmed rose at the discount store and give it to Ruthie to present to her mother.

"Hey, Sweetums," Ellen beamed in appreciation, her arms around Ruthie and her eyes acknowledging Bitty. "A yellow rose, huh?" Sitting Ruthie down, she peered into her friend's eyes. "Think we can make it through the next hurdle, Beatrice?"

Two scant months found Ellen readying herself for the start of classes. She hadn't heard from Jeffrey. Not even an occasional check arrived in the mail as she and Ruthie struggled to survive. She sought grants, worked as many hours as she could at the shoe store, and found herself sitting more and more at the dining room table trying to figure a way to make ends meet. With a sigh, she decided, Jeffrey had two years. Now he would have to face a guardian of the court to see that he made support payments for Ruthie. She prayed, asking God if Jeffrey would help now; in years to come he would not have to. With great trepidation, she searched her heart for an answer, knowing if Jeffrey refused to provide money for his daughter, he would suffer the consequences.

How many times had she riffled through the closet, aware the clothes she wore to work at the shoe store were less than stylish? The only thing that saved her was her taste ran more to classic tailored items than the frivolous fashion of the moment. Maybe she looked like an attorney or spinster schoolmarm, but Mr. Shumaker did not complain. In fact, sometimes she wondered if Mr. Shumaker even knew his employees' names.

"You, miss, help the young man up front." Or, "You're needed up front."

If Jenny, the college student, was working, or Jason, the twenty year old who said he couldn't find another job or he would not be selling shoes, they would glance toward each other, and then toward Mr. Shumaker, trying to make connection to whom he was speaking.

"It certainly wasn't Jason, was it?" Jenny would whisper. And if Mr. Shumaker had left the room, Jenny would don her best Segal voice, point a finger at Ellen and say, "Are you talkin' to me?" A few smiles along the way helped them get through the hours.

Fourth of July came and went. Ellen took Ruthie to the swimming pool when possible. Completely unaware of the turning of heads by the young males, Ellen sat beneath an umbrella and studied while Ruthie played in the shallow kids' pool. If she could have a head start, she knew it would serve her well. Unbeknownst to Ellen, with shapely legs and a summer tan, by the end of the month, Ellen's world was filled with admirers, though it was Ruthie who was lavished with attention.

"I like that John-boy," Ruthie chirped and talked as they drove back home on their last day at the pool. "He doesn't come all the time, but he asked me what you do, Mommy."

Bringing her thoughts back to Ruthie, Ellen asked, "What did you tell him?"

"I said you sell shoes for Mr. Shumaker, work at the hospital, and take care of me."

"That's a pretty good answer," Ellen grinned, reaching over to tousle Ruthie's hair.

School began. Bitty came daily. Ellen divided time between school and work. "There's promise, in you, Mrs. Anderson," Mrs. McCallister said. "How would you like to shadow one of the RN's over at Memorial?"

Ellen realized only a few were allowed to make rounds with the nursing staff at the hospital.

She had to think quickly, so as not to leave the instructor thinking she didn't appreciate the offer. "Umm," she cleared her throat, "I have a little daughter. I will have to be certain I have someone to stay with her."

"I see." Mrs. McCallister studied her student. "It gets a bit crazy trying to make all the rounds, doesn't it?"

Relieved, Ellen sighed. "Yes, ma'am, it does. I appreciate any information that has to do with changing schedules."

"I'll see what I can do." Mrs. McCallister started to leave. "I had two children to care for, when I began nursing school." She smiled. "Just keep on doing what you are now."

"Got any new instructions for me?" Bitty asked one morning.

Ellen stopped, closing her eyes a moment, thinking. "Just keep on doing what you are now."

Before they realized it, summer lapsed into cooler weather, and the leaves began to fall. *You can smell it in the air,* Bitty thought, *fall is upon us and Anne will be staying more nights.* By now they had all met Anne's little son, with haunting eyes like his momma peering out into the world. Bitty wondered, what kind of man could that boy's daddy be?

Maybe one like Ruthie's daddy, she surmised. She'd seen Ellen's sample letter, as she had seen bits and pieces Ellen had written to

Jeffrey asking for help. As far as Bitty knew, nothing had come of the letters. Ellen's grant supplied a certain amount to be used for child care, but nothing over the amount she insisted on paying Bitty.

Now, strained to breaking point, Ellen must feel she was doing what life required.

Wind rattled down the chimney and shook the upstairs windows. A light snow had started to fall mid-afternoon. Bitty was glad today was Thursday. On Thursday's she didn't have to go into the newspaper office or roll papers. Once the Wednesday paper with all the advertisements and coupons were out, the route people took over. Yes sir, today was her day off. She could stay in with Ruthie and enjoy the warmth. In the beginning, she worried about taking Ruthie with her, but Ellen said it was all right. "It will toughen her up." Bitty was always careful with Ruthie anyway.

"Where are you?" She called up the stairs as she pushed the vacuum cleaner out of sight into the hall closet. Then she realized Ruthie was in the living room.

"I'm in here, counting my pennies." Ruthie glanced up as Bitty entered. "Ever since Mommy said I could have the money laying around, I've found more."

Yawning, Bitty sank onto the sofa in front of Ruthie. She had a heap of money. Bitty grinned. She didn't know who found more pleasure in losing coins, her or Ellen.

"You got a bunch, haven't you? We'll go shopping one of these days, for sure."

"Have I got enough to buy Mommy a scarf?" Ruthie's eyes solemn and bright were pinned on Bitty. "She has to go out in the cold. She needs one."

Bitty stared at the pile of coins, her eyes squinting as she counted. "Maybe a few more." She would have to remember that when she made her rounds of the house.

Ruthie bounced up and ran to the window. "Look, Bitty, it's coming down really fast now."

Yes, it is, Bitty agreed silently, and her mind turned to Ellen. By the clock on the wall, Ellen would be finishing class and ready to go to the shoe store. Bitty glanced down the street. Not iced yet, but the snow was clinging. Ellen's house was on an incline, nearly top of the hill. Too much of this and she would have to leave her car on the back lot and walk across. Funny how the developers had been able to cut into the hill and level it for a parking lot that seldom had room for an extra car, but if it was snowing, Bitty thought there would be people leaving early to be sure they got home tonight.

"Will you stay?" Ruthie's voice was filled with excitement. "Mommy won't let you go home if it's dang-ros."

"*Dangerous.*" Bitty corrected. "Now let me see, that reminds me. What have we learned today?"

Ruthie ran to the piano where her mother kept a Bible. "Here, read this and we can learn something."

"There's the story of the sheep. A story about a widow."

"Are you a widow?" Ruthie thought for a moment. "I heard Mommy say she wasn't really a widow, but you were. What's a widow?"

"A widow is a woman who has lost her husband."

"Then Mommy must be one, too." Ruthie nodded. "She tried to call Daddy last night. I think we need money, and he is supposed to send it for me, but he doesn't."

Bitty was out of her element. She didn't know Ellen was that hard-pressed.

"I heard her say, 'He's gone? You think to Florida?' Where's Florida?"

"It is pretty far. About two days' drive, if you rest in between," Bitty replied.

Ruthie took the Bible. "Let me open it and where it opens is where we will read." She laughed. "I can't read, yet, but Mommy does that sometime when she says she needs advice. Let me show you. Hold it just like this, and it falls open to advice."

"I don't know." Bitty studied the page. "It's about a prodigal son."

"Read it." Ruthie's expression was solemn. "It's advice. It will help."

When Bitty finished, she sat with the Bible in her hands, wondering what would come next. There were a lot of prodigals in the world nowadays, to her way of thinking.

"Nope. That wasn't our advice," Ruthie quipped, slipping off the couch. "We don't have any money, except these pennies extra, and I never did run away."

"That settles that then, doesn't it?" Still, Bitty tucked that story away to think on later. "Don't you think we better check on that pot of soup on the burner?"

"Just a minute." Ruthie ran to look out the window. "Cool. It's white outside."

Everyone was rushing from the building. Classes had ended for the day, while outside the world they had seen upon arriving was now blanketed in white.

"Go on," Ellen insisted. "I'll be home after work." Worriedly, she scanned the sky. Snow had been falling for hours now. The streets were covered, even though the city trucks had been distributing salt since noon. She scrubbed the snow away from the windshield as Anne huddled beside her holding her book bag. "Just go, or call Bitty if you want." She sighed, removing a sodden glove from her right hand, and reached for the car's door handle. "Mercy. I forgot how cold it can get."

Anne pressed her cell phone into Ellen's hand. "If I'm going to your house, then you take the phone so if you have any trouble you can find help." Ellen started to protest.

"I mean it, Ellen. If I'm going to your house, you take the phone."

They each entered their cars to pull out of parking and onto the street. Anne's old battered car was heavier and made the turn nicely. Ellen's car was not only small but light, and she skidded onto the pavement, finally to straighten out as she stayed in the ruts made by other travelers' tires. The miles' drive to work was without incident, but she wondered later how she made it at all.

"See you made it." Jenny was stacking new arrivals when she entered the front. "Mr. Shumacher has gone home. Elvis is out of the building," she joked, "and Jason is due any minute. Think you two can hold down the fort? It's time for me to leave." Glancing out into the mall, Jenny shook her head in amazement. "Wouldn't you think those senior citizens would go home? I declare, Washington Mall always has the old guys on bad weather days." She giggled. "I guess the young folk are kept home by the parents." She stared at Ellen as she rummaged in her bag. "What are you doing?"

"Oh, I need to call home." She had been so intent, driving, she had forgotten she had Anne's phone. She dialed quickly. "Bitty, has Anne arrived? Good. Now, Bitty, the roads are terrible, please stay over so I won't have to worry over you." She smiled as she flipped the cell's cover. "My budget won't allow me one of these modern miracles."

"Then how does your friend have one?" Ellen didn't reply, because she knew Anne qualified through some government poverty plan. Jenny might not understand.

"I guess that means your baby sitter is staying?" Jenny was wrapping a wool scarf around her neck. In the long gray coat and black leather gloves, she was ready to face the wind. "Well, I'm out of here, toots."

The late evening hours waned into night, and Jason never arrived. Ellen had the store all to herself. Business was slow in the shoe store, but she noticed the Book Gallery was doing great business. She had just finished straightening and was returning from the back with an assortment of bags when she heard someone say, "Excuse me, miss."

Her heart made a remarkable thump in her chest. "Oh, I didn't realize anyone was here."

"Didn't mean to scare you." A man was rising from behind one of the aisles. "Evening, ma'am."

Ellen's eyes followed up to his, deep set, heavily lashed, the deepest blue one could imagine. Mentally, she shook herself. It was the cobalt scarf around his neck that brought out the color, no doubt. Faintly mocking, he was waiting her assessment.

"Good evening," he said again.

Ellen struggled for composure. "Yes. Good evening. May I help you?" She had noticed his words more drawn out than the Northern twang of the regulars, almost a drawl.

"I need a pair of boots," he was saying. "I'm visiting home, and I'm afraid I didn't think to bring boots." He smiled. "Actually, I travel light, and a pair the size to fit me would have needed their own suitcase."

"And that size would be?"

"Let's try a twelve. I plan to wear thick socks."

Moving behind the aisle, she scanned for a size twelve. "Do you want oiled leather that will stand up to the elements, or were you thinking of rubber boots? I'm afraid we don't carry those, but McNas down the hall does."

He was speaking again. She heard him say leather. Something about where he came from they didn't need snow boots, but a lot of the guys wore western boots, in fact he had several pair back home. It was almost magnetizing, the slow fluid drawl of his speech. She felt as though she had been dropped into a barrel of oil, wanting to languish there. He was standing over her. He was very tall and muscular she supposed, if one could tell beneath the long black coat. His hair was black as well, and the faintest shadow of beard was obvious above the blue scarf.

Wordlessly, she handed over the box. "Size twelve. Treated leather."

He nodded. "Good. I was afraid you wouldn't have my size." He removed the long coat, tossing it onto the opposite row of chairs, and sat down. Untying the shoe strings, long fingers tidied up the socks, finally pulled the boots on first one foot, then the other. "Isn't this where you tug and push and tell me I need a different size?" That smooth voice mocked her, as his smile had done.

Brought once more to cognizance, Ellen grinned. She had been studying his clothing. Blue-gray collar-less shirt, gray pleated trousers, and a small silver cross around his neck, all nicely done. Brooks Brothers, she assumed. At least. Or maybe that line of trousers Dave Letterman wore. Self-consciously she glanced down at her own dated suit. Driving had required a bit more time in the snow. She had thrown on the silk mauve blouse, clasped a string of pearls around her neck, donned the gray knee-length skirt and the matching jacket, and hurried into work. Mr. Shumacher had agreed to her use of a small dressing room in the back and even installed a small oval mirror, she suspected so she could do something with her hair. Today, of all days, she had let it fall onto her shoulders, brushing it once before going out onto the floor.

"Do you need to stand up and walk? See if they're comfortable?"

"Like a juvenile?" He smiled back. "Actually, I believe they are fine. Everything is fine."

Ellen blushed as his eyes ran the length of her body. Was he actually studying her as she had him, or were her hormones a wreck and it was her imagination? Not in the three years, since she left Jeffrey's bed, had Ellen thought of another man. It must be the weather. That had to be it. She was on a one-way course, to further her career and take care of Ruthie all by herself; there would be no detours along the way.

As she rang up the sale, she sensed he had a question, following his gaze as he stared out the window. When she handed him the bag, he tilted his head to one side as if deciding, and then walked briskly toward the door ... and as abruptly turned and came back to where she waited, a serious expression on his face.

"I was thinking, it's mighty cold out there, and the streets are pretty much iced over. Do you have adequate transportation to get home?" A small frown wrinkled his brow. "I apologize. I just thought if you didn't, I rented a four-wheel drive, and I could ..."

The tingling that had raced along her spine eased. Ellen's friendly smile shone as she interrupted, "Thank you. I really do have transportation to get home." She sighed. "It is nice of you to ask."

He straightened the scarf around his neck, patted the front of the black coat, and smiled in return. "If you are sure."

"I am." She glanced at the clock over the door. Five minutes past closing. People were filling up the halls. The parking lot would be busy by now with shoppers leaving. Her customer was heading out Shumacher's door.

She closed the shop. Hurrying to her car, she did not see the black Suburban that followed her out of the parking lot. Nor was she aware, when she turned onto the street to begin a precarious climb up the hill, the Suburban waited.

"Atta girl," Garcia nodded agreement when she backed the short distance down and watched as she parked in a lot behind what must have been near her home.

Full house awaited Ellen's arrival. Bitty, Anne, and Ruthie were seated around the dining room table. She saw them as she unloaded the book bag, her coat, and purse on the hook and small shelf by the front door and hurried in to join them. "Wow. You have it warm and toasty in here." The usual joyous excitement Ruthie expounded upon her arrival was not forthcoming. "What's wrong?"

"We have company." Ruthie pointed to the living room, even as Anne and Bitty placed index fingers over their lips.

"It's a joke." Ellen smiled, going along with the game. "Is it Santa? Because if it is, he is early. As in e-a-r-l-y," she spelled.

Ruthie climbed down from the chair, motioned for Ellen to bend down, and clasp her arms around her mother's neck. "She's in there. She said she had already eat."

"*Eaten*," Ellen corrected. "So, it is Mrs. Claus?" Ellen picked up Ruthie, giving her a resounding smooch on the forehead. "Well, then, let's just go see this Mrs. Claus." She stopped short at the door to the living room, however. There sat Mrs. Harriet Becker, their next door neighbor, the one who made it clear she didn't like little children and didn't want them trespassing on her lawn, bothering her dog, or asking for favors. Ellen and Bitty had honored her request with a vengeance. "Mrs. Becker," Ellen managed. "What a surprise."

"I hope you don't mind, Ellen." Mrs. Becker spoke as though they talked every day. In fact, they rarely spoke as Mrs. Becker avoided them completely.

"My furnace quit. The repairman said he will come tomorrow to fix it, if he can get up the hill." Drawing a deep breath, Mrs. Becker concluded. "He says there are many people without heat tonight. I can't imagine why; they should have known when the snow started falling to prepare, of course. A furnace stopping is not comparable."

"Of course not," Ellen was groping for sensibility as to how to arrange for Mrs. Becker to sleep. But Mrs. Becker had thought that over too. As Ellen stared at her neighbor, Mrs. Becker pointed to a stack of blankets by the side of the sofa.

"If it is all right, I brought my own covers, if I may use your sofa tonight."

"What an unusual night," Ellen whispered to Anne and Bitty as they walked up the stairs together and reached the hall's landing that led off to Ruthie's room.

"What's unusal mean?" a groggy Ruthie asked from the safety of her mother's arms.

"*Different.*" The three women chortled together and then burst into giggles.

"All right, you two." Ellen gave them a stern gaze. "Lights out and no giggling."

"You want me to fix breakfast in the morning?" Bitty asked.

"Nope. If me and Anne can get down the hill in her car, it will be business as usual." Ellen grinned. "That leaves you to take care of our neighbor and Ruthie. You sure you two can share a bed? Seeing as how the couch is taken?" Ellen was certain they were considering the circumstances that brought Mrs. Becker into their circle, just as she was, but soon the house settled down to its age old squeaks and groans, Ruthie nestled close, and sleep claimed them for a short night's rest.

>—<

"How did you sleep?" Ellen stopped by the open door to the hall bathroom.

"Man, I'm glad you talked me into leaving a few necessities here. I can't stand not brushing my teeth. It's kind of like a sanity check. If I ever quit …" her voice trailed off.

"Do you suppose Mrs. Becker brought hers?"

Anne giggled. "As for sleep, you don't even know Bitty's there. She sleeps on the very edge of the bed and never moves. Now, Mrs. Becker I could hear snoring all the way down stairs."

"Guess you didn't sleep well, huh?"

"Not bad. While I was growing up, we had cousins in and out, guess who they slept with? I can adjust to about anything." Anne searched a small cosmetic bag for a pin.

"I thought you were an only child."

"I was, but Harley's sister had a bunch of kids, and just like he helped me, he was always helping them too. Mom was pretty much unaware of anything, even then. She drank her wine and went to bed. My stepdad saw to most all our needs."

"Some things don't change, do they?" Ellen sighed. "Like me and you, fending for ourselves." She shook her head, remembering. "Life with Jeffrey was that way."

"Where did you say he is now?"

"Don't know for sure." Ellen shrugged. "I tried calling. We really could use a little cash for Christmas." She grimaced. "But the person who answered the phone said he had moved, left no forwarding address. Still, she heard he and his girlfriend married and had moved to Florida." Ellen watched Anne wad her hair on top of her head, push a pin through it, just as she had. The instructor wanted their hair pinned up. "Grapevine stuff, the woman said, just what she heard."

"I'm so sorry." Anne laid a hand on Ellen's arm. "You have enough problems without me staying here so much."

"Shush." Ellen reached for Anne's hand and started out of the room. "Come on, with the icy roads, we both better pray your car makes it down this hill."

→ ←

CLASS LET OUT BY TWO thirty. Anne dropped Ellen in the parking lot behind the house. While Ellen didn't have time to stop in to see Ruthie, she saw them wave to her from the upstairs window. Ruthie threw a kiss, and she made an exaggerated effort in showing she caught it. Her car coughed and sputtered before the motor finally settled to a rumble; maybe she could make it downtown since the snow had thawed a bit from traffic. They knew her schedule. She would be home sometime after nine, depending on how busy the shop was and if the pavement had not frozen into ice again. As she drove, she thought about Jeffrey marrying again and wondered if it was the woman he dated while they were married. Even before the divorce, there had been nothing between them. He said it was his business. He had to spend every waking moment to keep it going. Early morning hours he left; late night sometimes he returned. The pattern to their marriage was Jeffrey coming home awhile, evenings, to watch sports and then leaving. Ellen worried over the books. The hours Jeff spent working somehow were not justified. They hardly paid the bills. It was during that time her parents, who lived in a nearby town, had cautioned, "People in construction do not leave their beds at two o'clock in the morning, Ellie. You best be watching your husband, or else one day you'll be standing on the sideline with nothing to your name."

Ellen regretted the words spoken between them. All their caution had come to fruition. And not once had she considered perhaps they knew something she did not. What she denied and dared not consider, in the beginning, she came to realize, was true. By then, she had severed ties with her family. She hoped Ruthie was too little to remember those days with Jeffrey. He hardly recognized his child's presence. From the time Ruthie could walk, she would climb up to sit as close as possible by his side. Fathering instincts were not a part of Jeffrey Anderson's makeup.

Once Bitty had asked, "What about your parents? Will they be visiting soon?"

Ellen replied hastily, "We don't correspond." Though Bitty's mouth formed a thin line, she never questioned again. Time had lapsed. No need stirring up old feelings. She sighed, pulling into the mall parking lot. If her parents knew what she had been through, their hearts would turn inside out. And if they knew how sweet Ruthie was … she shivered, whether from the cold or inner yearnings, Ellen didn't know. Sometimes she wished she could return home to Mom and Dad and feel their arms around her. From the guilt that lay within her, she felt she must prove herself to them, and she would, once she finished the nursing program.

Entering the shop, without any preamble, her thoughts returned to the man in the shoe store last night. Jenny was busy, dusting shelves, using a cloth to polish the toes of shoes, a flutter of energy, Ellen surmised, and she wondered why Mr. Shumacher kept silent vigil near the front door.

"I'm leaving on time," Jenny whispered. "That one there is mad as all get out that Jason didn't show last night."

"But the roads were really bad." She thought of the one customer.

"Whatever." Jenny's eyes darted sideways to be certain of Mr. Shumacher's location. "That doesn't mean the young man couldn't call," she imitated in a staunch whisper.

"There was hardly any business. Looks to me like he'd be glad Jason didn't show."

"Go figure." Jenny's eyes were on the clock. "I'm out of here." She headed toward the back, turning. "Psst." She motioned Ellen near. "There's a credit card in the drawer, I don't think Mr. Shumacher has noticed. It must have been left here last night. I'm thinkin' you better call the owner," her eyes turned toward their boss, "before he sees it."

"But I only had one customer. I'm certain he paid cash."

"Whatever." Jenny sighed. "It was in the back group of chairs."

Ellen called the credit card company. There was no address on the card. Of course, they were the only ones that could locate Daniel Gates, whose last four numbers on the card were eight nine four two. No, she had never met the man before. No, she had not found his name in the phone book, and yes, she would hold the card until hearing from Mr. Gates. If not today, then she would comply by mailing the card to the company.

Eight o'clock arrived. Mr. Shumacher prepared to leave, ready to go through the door when Daniel Gates appeared. Ellen breathed in sharply. He was every bit as handsome as she thought. The long black coat was gone. Instead, he was wearing denims, a fringed leather jacket, and the boots she sold him last night. The muscles in her stomach tightened as he sauntered into the room, the finger of one hand looped into the back pocket of his jeans.

"Why, Daniel, you rascal." Mr. Shumacher extended one hand, gripping Daniel Gates's firmly as he eyed him up and down. "Haven't seen you in years, though your Aunt Georgia tells me you've been making a name for yourself." He gave a nod, seeming to approve of the younger man. "Textiles, in California?"

"That's right."

While Ellen looked on, the two conversed, swapping tidbits. Feeling a bit uncomfortable, and wondering if he would mention the card before Mr. Shumacher left, she pointed toward the cash register and then busied herself with replacing boxes left askew on the floor.

"I'll not keep you, Dan." Mr. Shumacher pulled on expensive leather gloves. "You come by the house if you have time this visit."

"Yes, sir. I surely will."

They met at the counter. He laid his hands on the edge, leaned forward, and smiled at her.

"I got a call, Ellen, saying you have something of mine. Is that right?"

He was completely aware of the slight flush to her face as she opened the cash drawer and drew out the card. Studying her, he noticed the way her eyes had deepened. Long lashes curled above indescribable color. He was mesmerized watching them change to an unforgettable amber belying turbulent emotion and hidden passion. Today she wore a soft brown pinstriped suit, a crème colored shirt that appeared to be made of satin, and the same strand of pearls. He would not understand, later, the instinctive desire to see her hair tumbling onto her shoulders and was amazed at himself when he leaned over and pulled the tortoise pick from her hair. She blushed, her hand coming up to touch his, and her eyes deepened even more.

"You are a very beautiful lady," he said in a gentle admiring voice.

"Thank you." Ellen glanced away. What could she say? Her insides were churning. Surely he could see that one touch had completely disoriented her. She commanded her brain to function, holding the card in midair. His hand closed over hers.

Savoring the moment, taking his time, he finally said, "Thank you." Reluctant to loosen his hold, his eyes held hers, direct, questioning. "I must have had it in my back pocket again. After this, I will try not to do that."

Ellen swallowed. This was crazy. It was just a card. No, it wasn't the card. It was the rush of feeling she saw reflected back in his eyes. She knew he was as amazed as she by what they were experiencing. *And what exactly was that?*

"Let me introduce myself," he said. "I am Daniel Gates. Mr. Shumacher lives near my aunt, whom I am visiting."

"Ellen Anderson."

"Mrs. Anderson, by any chance?" He wore a curiously sincere expression as he asked.

"There is no longer a Mr. Anderson. He recently remarried."

"That's good, isn't it?" he questioned, noticing the withdrawal of her hand.

She shrugged. "It was never up to me. Mr. Anderson always chose."

"Hmmm." He rubbed his chin, eyes squinting, as he evaluated the information. "I'd say Mr. Anderson was a fool."

Ellen felt as though some primitive instinct had taken hold of her mind and body. "And is there a Mrs. Gates?"

He grinned mischievously. "I thought you would never ask." He stepped back, hands in the pockets of his jeans, and studied her. "There has never been a Mrs. Gates. I came close one time, but she threw me over for a man with money."

Ellen snorted. "Sorry," she gave a feeble apology. "Somehow I doubt that."

Dan feigned hurt. "You would doubt my word?"

Enjoying the sparring, Ellen grinned. "Not your word, perhaps, but the …"

Dan laughed. "I know. I was surprised too. But, then, I had no money."

He was remarkable. Ellen was smitten by his laughter, by the way the little lines crinkled at the corner of his eyes, that a man as large as he would enjoy such trivial banter with a stranger such as herself.

"Well, Miss Ellen Anderson, I will be in town through the holidays. Do you think you …?" He paused. "How do I say this? Would you feel inclined to join me in a social nuance to which I've already been invited?" He grinned. "And I'm sure there will be more."

For a moment Ellen looked away, avoiding his eyes as she toyed with a notepad left lying on the counter. "I … ah."

He noticed her color had paled a bit.

"I work so many hours, and I have a little daughter that I spend any spare time with."

"And?" He tilted his head, studying her again. "Which of those would prevent your accompanying me on a few social events, usually after a small child's bedtime hour?" Suddenly concerned, he added, "There are baby sitters, aren't there? You do have help?"

Tears brimmed in her eyes. "I have wonderful help."

As he backed away, Dan lifted one hand to his forehead, a sort of salute. "You can think about it, then. I'll be back to see what you decide." Deep laughter sounded in his throat as he left. "You better decide to help me out, Miss Anderson."

The next evening, when Mr. Shumacher informed Jenny and Ellen that Jason was no longer an employee, for once Jenny remained quiet. Ellen chewed her lip, nervously afraid Mr. Shumacher would ask her to work Jason's shift. And she kicked herself, inwardly; only a week earlier she had said if he needed her, she could use the hours. Now, with a date pending, she had become another person, forgetting the money that was needed.

"Where is the fair-haired boy?" Jenny asked.

"Florida," Shumacher replied in a disgusted voice as he walked away.

Behind Shumacher's back, Jenny raised an arm high. "Yes," she mouthed quietly when their boss was well out of hearing distance. "Way to go, Jason. I could use a little of that Florida sunshine myself."

CHAPTER 4

THE STREETS WERE WORSE THAN the night before. Ellen noticed Anne had made it up the hill, and there was a large Suburban parked a short distance from her car and the gate that led from the parking lot to her yard. She had heard a short news report that the utility company feared the lines bringing electricity to homes in the city might fall. "That's all we need," she mumbled out loud, momentarily wondering about the likelihood of Mrs. Becker's furnace being repaired that day, or for that matter the stability of the one in her own ninety-five-year-old house. "Please," she glanced up toward the sky, knowing only by the grace of God had she made it up the hill. "Please, don't fail me now."

Bitty met her as she opened the door.

"What's wrong, Bitty?" She saw the worried look on the baby sitter's face. "Is something wrong with Ruthie? Is she sick?"

"No." Bitty clasp her hands together, fairly wringing them red. "Come, see." She led Ellen down the stairs, to the basement, and stood in front of the washer. "It won't work. I don't know what's wrong with it, but it won't even turn the motor." To demonstrate, Bitty turned the dial on the top of the washer and waited while nothing happened.

Ellen sank down on the lid of a plastic detergent bucket. "So the washer finally quit." She sighed, letting her face fall forward into her hands. "I guess things can't last forever, can they?" Her voice was muffled behind splayed fingers. "And here I was thinking what if the furnace quit."

Clearing her throat, Bitty said, "You probably won't want to hear this, but Mrs. Becker is still upstairs. The man couldn't come today, too many house calls, more work than he had imagined, she said."

"I wondered about that. It's really bad out there. I was afraid I couldn't get home from the mall."

"I thought classes might dismiss and you would come home early."

"Bitty, I'm sorry I didn't call." She glanced up. Miserably upset, she was already wondering how to afford a new washer with Christmas near. "I thought Anne would tell you when she arrived."

"Anne?"

"Didn't Anne come here?"

"Haven't seen hide nor hair of that girl since this morning when you both left."

"Her car is in the parking lot." Worry crept into Ellen's voice. "Where's Ruthie?"

"You won't believe this either." Shaking her head, Bitty said, "She's up there sitting by Mrs. Becker on the couch, and both of them sound asleep."

Pale-cheeked, and dark-eyed, Ellen was in a whir over Anne's absence, but this, Mrs. Becker and her baby cuddled up together, boggled the mind.

A sound, somewhere between a sob and laughter, melded together as it came out of her throat. "This I'll have to see." Pushing up off the bucket, Ellen touched Bitty's shoulder. "Thanks, Bitty, for being here with Ruthie. I don't know what I'd do without you."

"Won't be any charge for this week, Ellen. Me stranded here with you. It's the least I can do." She turned to follow Ellen up the steps. "Besides, I love Ruthie."

A smile flitted across Ellen's face, fading as she glanced out the window. Streetlights cast yellowed beams across the iced street. "A person could freeze to death out there."

"You think something has happened to Anne?" Bitty asked as they stared at each other. "The telephone hasn't rung all afternoon."

Turning, they hurried into the hall. Ellen picked up the receiver and listened. "It's dead. We wouldn't know if someone tried to call." She pulled a heavy hooded coat from the coat rack. "I'm going out to the parking lot and look around. I don't really know what to look for, but we have to start somewhere."

The wind chill factor had to be near zero. Wind was sweeping the dried snow into drifts, and water was hard frozen. She noticed the Suburban was gone, but Anne's old car sat in the same location. Scrubbing a spot on the window, she peered inside. Only Anne's back pack lay in the driver's seat, books spilled into the floorboard. Stepping away from the car, she peered around the parking lot. The only activity was the driving force of the wind. Nothing stirred. It wasn't like Anne. She kept her cell phone close. Anne would have called, unless something or someone prevented her doing so.

Turning and bracing herself against the wind, Ellen began to make her way back to the house. Dimly aware of car lights beaming across her path, she could only wonder that anyone would be out in such blizzard force. She pulled the hood tightly around her face and searched for the gate opening. It was only when she stepped inside the yard she thought she heard someone calling. Fumbling with the metal lock, she tried to push the gate back open, but the wind increased, causing the unevenness of the fence sides to tighten and hold the gate firmly shut.

Two men appeared, one on each side of a huddled form. "Miss. Miss."

Her first thought was to run, but something held her captive to the insistence in their voices. She stared hard through the gates widened cracks. Something familiar touched her mind. But she could only question why they would appear to be dragging the third person along. Then she heard the faintest calling of her name. A woman's voice was saying, "Ellen."

"Anne?"

"Miss?" We are police officers."

She could barely see, but the badges, the black leather jackets, and the caps with ear muffs seemed to be present... and Anne. Tiny, frail, little Anne, her friend appeared even more diminished in size between the two officers. One braced himself and pulled the gate wide enough that the second could pass through with Anne. Huddled and tightly wrapped in a green army blanket, Anne reached out to Ellen, her hands trembling and cold. Ellen saw Anne was crying. Fear was gone; in its place, relief. Ellen pulled Anne into her arms.

"Anne. What happened?"

"Could we step into your house?" one of the men asked. He held up a badge she could see by the snow's reflection from a streetlamp across the way, but the numbers were lost in the darkness. "I'm Officer Cullens. This is my partner, Officer Glenn Hankins. She's cold, and we need to get her inside so she can get out of those wet clothes."

"It's all right, Ellen." Anne's teeth chattered as she tried to speak, the words coming out in a hoarse whisper. "They really are police officers. They found me."

"I have a small child inside," Ellen explained. "Please do not frighten her."

"No, ma'am."

Thankfully Ellen heard the gentle wisp of snoring coming from the front room, and Ruthie was still snuggled next to their neighbor. Bitty came forward, wisely and gently taking Anne in tow to lead her upstairs. "There's coffee on the stove," she said.

Taking two heavy mugs from the nearest cabinet, Ellen motioned for the two officers to step into the dining room. "We can talk in there," she said, pouring coffee into the cups and handing them to the men, who accepted them appreciatively.

"We wanted to take her to headquarters, but she insisted we bring her here."

"Yes." Ellen slid onto the chair at the end of the table. "With the weather, Anne has been staying a few days, whenever she needs, because she lives a good distance south of here."

"Does Miss Graves have any reason to suspect someone has a vendetta against her?"

"Why would you ask that?"

"We found her on the side of the road, ma'am. Obviously someone beat her up pretty badly, or the fall onto the road … you get the picture, I'm sure."

Ellen blanched. "Anne is the most gentle soul in the world."

"Still, she said someone grabbed her as she was walking toward the gate to your property, and that the person threw something over her head and dragged her to a vehicle."

"Was she physically harmed?" Visions of someone, she knew not who, raping Anne nauseated Ellen. "She was so dirty and visibly shaken, I thought it best that Bitty take her upstairs and get her cleaned up, settled down."

"No," the officer gave a deep sigh. "I think someone didn't want her to know who they were and roughed her up, then threw her out before she realized who he was."

"Definitely a man. Is that what Anne said? One person?"

"Yes." The second officer spoke quietly, aware of the two sleeping in the other room. "Could there be a case of mistaken identity, ma'am? I mean, with Miss Graves staying with you?"

"Me?" *Ludicrous*, Ellen thought. *Who would mean to harm me?* "That's ridiculous."

"Ma'am." Officer Cullen glanced to his partner and back to Ellen, seeming reluctant to say what was on his mind. "If either of you ladies have anything in your past, we," he paused momentarily, "we, ah, can run your names and find that information."

"Let me get this straight," Ellen bristled. "You find Anne on the side of the road, abused, Lord only knows why, and you ask if we have records?" She pinned a hostile glare on both men. "The only thing you will find on Anne, or me, is this. We are both divorced from husbands who could care less if we are mauled, mugged, or whatever." Her shoulders heaved with anger. "We each have a small child. Anne's son stays weekdays with her former husband, the child's father. My child is with me one hundred percent. I have a sitter who guards her with her life." Ellen had risen while speaking and was now pacing the floor between the table where the two men sat and the adjoining room. She was dangerously wondering if she had the right to ask them to leave ... or better still throw them out the door herself.

"Excuse, me, ma'am." Officer Glenn Hankins stood suddenly, one hand outstretched. "I implore you, do not take our questions wrongly. Often the very situations you describe are enough to create this situation. We were not accusing you or Miss Graves of anything." He drew a deep breath. "It is our job to ask. Miss Graves strongly pleaded with us not to take her into headquarters, but to bring her here. Taking the condition of the weather into consideration, we did that."

It was late when the officers left, promising to return the next day, weather permitting. Bitty had worked miracles in the background, taking Ruthie up to Ellen's bed, thankful the child and the next door neighbor had eaten early in the evening because they could not be certain when Anne or Ellen would arrive home. Bitty, small as she was, had eased the larger buxom Mrs. Becker down on the sofa, with the woman not missing a beat in the rhythm of snores that emitted from her body. Somehow she had calmed Anne as she ran a bath and insisted a long soak in Ellen's old clawfoot tub was what would ease the aches and pains Anne was feeling from the blows and the cold to her body.

Then, like a guard watching over a beloved patron wrongly convicted, Bitty stood by the door, understanding Ellen's anger. Resolutely aware, Bitty realized more was at stake here than the police officers were saying. It was this comprehension Bitty accepted as divine intervention, beyond her own intelligence. She would be staying on, far longer than the ice on the streets or the wind that was now rattling down the chimney. Bitty knew Ellen would not mind, in fact would accept the gift of her presence for the sake of the small child they both loved. In moving, Bitty had stored more furniture than she used. With Lawrence gone, and no family to call her own, Ellen and Ruthie had filled that absence in her life. Ellen's home had a third floor. Perhaps it was only a finished attic, Bitty was not certain, but there was adequate room. When the thaw came, Bitty would put into motion the plan that was forming in her mind.

"A TREE. A TREE." RUTHIE clapped her hands together. "Just like Christ Church."

"The church we see on television, welcoming people," Bitty explained.

"It's nearly bigger than we can manage," Harriet admitted. "I guess I got a bit carried away. When the boy said 'more for your money,' I ordered it." She puffed over to the sofa, pushed aside the cushions, and sat down. "I'll have to tread over to the house and find those decorations I haven't seen in years."

"What's decorations?" Ruthie was down on her knees watching Bitty placing an old curtain around the base of the tree. "Mommy said we used to put bright shiny balls on our tree, but I don't know."

"Those are ornaments," Harriet nodded. "I ask Ellen if she had decorations, and she said she was afraid they got lost in the shuffle, after the d-i-v-o-r-c-e," Harriet spelled.

"Div ..." Appearing perplexed, Ruthie tried sounding the letters.

"You're too smart for your own good," Harriet chuckled. "Now," rising from the sofa, she wiped her hands on the sides of the sweatshirt she was wearing and asked, "what's next?"

"Ornaments," Ruthie shouted. "Right, Bitty? She said ornaments."

"And we better hurry; the truck with the furniture from storage is supposed to be here by ten o'clock." Bitty said, glancing toward the stairs. "That should be fun."

"I declare, there's nothing like Christmas with a little child in the midst of it all," Harriet exclaimed. "I tell you, Bitty, I've been shut off from the world so long, all that's going on now seems like a fairy tale."

"You said Jesus sounds like a fairy tale," Ruthie remembered. "Mommy says he's not."

"I'm sorry about that, Ruthie. Perhaps I shouldn't have said it."

To Bitty, Harriet continued, "I've had too many Christmases alone, since George Becker died. Who would believe I'd be sharing this one with a group of women?" Staring hard at the floor, she admitted, "I know I should have gone to a hotel, but I came here, like an intruder, casting myself upon Ellen and your goodness, Bitty."

Bitty's hands stilled. "It's a whole new world here, isn't it? Different from our raising ... both girls with little ones and no husband to speak of. We were expected to stay with our man, no matter what." Hearing a sound, she turned to the window. "Why, they're early. It's only nine. Here comes the bed, Ruthie. I hope they will carry it up those stairs; if not, we've got our job cut out for us."*

"No ma'am, we don't move it, just deliver it." Harriet gave her best imitation of the man who brought Bitty's furniture. Ruthie laughed and Bitty grinned. It was a tussle. Making the curve to the upstairs landing seemed nearly impossible. But they made it. Harriet's hair had become a frizz of tiny curls where sweat had formed around the hairline, and Bitty looked to be on her last leg.

"I didn't remember the headboard being this heavy."

"It's oak. Heavy oak." Harriet was examining the four poster. "Pretty, though."

"We will never get that dresser up these stairs without removing every drawer."

Which they did, requiring a number of trips up and down the stairs, until all was complete, right down to a lace runner on top of the dresser and Bitty's mother's lamps retrieved from her own car. She had never trusted putting precious things in storage.

"The room looks good." Harriet helped Bitty throw a chenille spread across the bed. "I didn't know they still made these. I've had a couple in my time, and I guess that's all my mother ever had." Her mind drifted away, coming back, staring at the voiles on the window. "You still intend to hang drapes that will pull over these sheers?" Stepping across the few feet between the bed and the window, she peered out.

"That black vehicle has been sitting there for days. And if it's not, I have seen an old van." She sighed. "It's not familiar to me. I don't believe it belongs around here." Pausing, she shook her head, "No, it came in with the snow storm." Movement caught her eye. "There he is, the guy with the funny little hat on his head." She laughed as she watched him bang on the driver side of the door and then walk around to open the passenger door and climb in. "He looks cold."

"I guess I thought that was a service van," Bitty replied, moving to stand beside Harriet at the window. "Anne said she thought she was in a van or truck of sorts, but only a fool would hang around for the cops to catch him."

"I'll get on over to the house and find those Christmas decorations; I sure hope I find them. Don't you, Ruthie?" She grinned, stopping to pat Ruthie's arm. "I bet your mommy will be surprised to see what all has been done."

"We are going to turn the lights out and hide when Mommy comes home, aren't we, Bitty? She will be so happy to see the tree and …" She stopped, a worried frown on her brow. "Do we have lights, Bitty? We have to have lights, don't we?"

"Yes, we do," Bitty comforted. "I bought new ones. They are downstairs in a sack. I just didn't know if we'd have a tree." She smiled. "I thought we could run them down the stair rail if we had to. But I'm not so sure we should hide and scare Mommy." Bitty thought they'd had enough scare over Anne's incident.

"Okay, but we can leave the room dark, and then when she sees it's dark, we can turn on the lights and surprise her." Ruthie bounced around the room. "Won't she be happy?"

Harriet returned to find Bitty making sandwiches and soup in the kitchen. "It's vegetable. I'll let it simmer until dinner tonight. What do you think?"

"Smells divine." Harriet wondered over the change she had witnessed in Bitty. She ran Ellen's house as efficiently as a skilled worker, watched over Ruthie with a happy intensity Harriet had not seen before, and still found time for rolling newspapers for the local office. Except with the bad weather, some man had called to tell Bitty he would see that her papers were taken care of and she was to stay in. In the beginning the two had eyed each other with mistrust, Bitty saying very few words to Harriet, and Harriet had a habit through the years of not trusting anyone, but who could remain quiet with Ruthie in their midst? The child had so much love to give and saw the world in such a way it made one want to participate. Harriet saw the struggle Ellen faced too. She wasn't quite clear on the prayers continually offered at the table at night, nor the daily reading of Scripture from the Bible either. She had asked Bitty, "Do you believe that stuff? Why do you do it?"

"Because Ellen believes it and she wants Ruthie to hear it."

That look of firmness she had come accustomed to in Bitty's person was enough; Harriet questioned no further. This was Ellen's home.

The house was dark as pitch when Ellen arrived home. No doubt something was in the making; when Ruthie and Bitty were up to something, they hid their work until it was completed. On the other hand, their lives had been shaken by what happened to Anne. All seemed normal on the outside, but inside it was as if they kept looking over their shoulders. Ellen shuddered, remembering the officers' questions. "Has anyone got a vendetta against either of you?"

Protection was left in Bitty's hands where Ruthie was concerned, and she trust Bitty completely. She had to go to work every day as though nothing had happened, and school was nonnegotiable. The quicker she had her license, life would be easier. If her grandmother's will had not provided enough money, they would be homeless. In her heart she knew, Jeffrey would have gone through her inheritance, if it had been settled while they were together. Still, she realized, Anne, Bitty, and herself wondered why Anne was taken and then thrown onto the highway. The cops questioned if it were possibly a case of mistaken identity. Ellen suspected Anne relived the situation in her mind daily as she fumbled through each hour.

"All I know," Anne said, "someone threw an old blanket over my head, wrestled me into a smelly old vehicle—I think it was a van—and sometime later shoved me out onto the street. None of it makes sense, but I will never forget that wild ride and the smell, and then as if for good measure, he kept punching me."

They went over it a million times. "Were you questioned?" she asked Anne.

Anne replied, "Not really. He seemed angry, like he'd made a mistake, but no questions. More like a silence, wondering what to do with me, and I was scared to death."

Now as she started up the steps, Ellen closed her mind to that night. She must. "Someone has all the curtains closed," she called out. "Anyone home?" A small hard body hit her knees as arms wrapped around her legs. "Aww, Sweetums, is that you?

"It's me. It's me." Giggling, Ruthie looked up. "Are you surprised?"

CHAPTER 5

"WHERE ARE YOU GOING?" Ruthie met her mother's eyes in the mirror. A slight pout of the mouth, and an accusing tone, told Ellen Ruthie was not happy. "Why can't I go?" Her daughter seemed to know something was different about tonight.

This was difficult. Ellen swallowed and returned the solemn scrutiny. Ruthie's cheeks were pink. She hoped she wasn't coming down with something, and Christmas only days away. What a week. She ran the tip of her tongue over her lips. "Do you like this color of lipstick?" Ruthie moved to stand between Ellen on the stool and the low vanity with mirror.

"I don't like lipstick." Reaching for her daughter, Ellen pulled Ruthie close to her chest. "You've had such a busy week, haven't you?" She waited for Ruthie to soften, but her body was still and stiff. Peering down into those solemn eyes so much like her own, Ellen smiled and then planted a kiss on Ruthie's forehead. "You and Bitty have worked on the attic room."

"Harriet helped."

"Yes, Miss Harriet helped."

"She said I can call her Harriet, too," Ruthie said crossly. "We're friends." Defiant now, she crossed her arms to her chest and explained. "Harriet said she is sorry she was mean to me when we moved in here and that she voided me always."

"That she always *avoided* you," Ellen corrected.

"That too."

"I thought this was the night you and Bitty and Miss Harriet were going to watch the Nativity on the Hallmark channel."

"I forgot." Ruthie snuggled close to her mother. "I like to sit on your lap. Your lap feels different than Miss Harriet's, and Bitty doesn't have much lap."

"I know." Ellen grinned, relieved that Ruthie was weakening. "You know something? I like the way you and Bitty decorated the house for Christmas. I like the tree."

"It's like Christ Church tree.

"What do you know about Christ Church having a tree?"

"Silly." Ruthie grinned. "When Dora rests, I see Christ Church. The man says, welcome to Christ Church, we welcome you to join us." Ruthie clapped her hands, "Then Dora comes back on. Bitty says its *andertiseunt*."

"*Advertisement*," Ellen corrected.

"That too." Ruthie nodded her head importantly. "They got a tree."

"We put the baby Jesus and his mother on the table in the living room so we can all see it. Miss Harriet ordered the tree." Ruthie wore a puzzled expression as she tilted her head to one side and said, "We never did order a Christmas tree on the telephone, did we?"

"No, we didn't."

"She did." Excitement was rising in Ruthie's voice. "She said, we want a tree as tall as the fireplace, don't we, Ruthie? And I said yes, and she said, all right. Then she went over to her house and brought all those red glass *ornsmet*, and we put them all over the tree."

"Ornaments."

"Yes." Ruthie's eyes sparkled. "Then when me and Bitty went shopping, we got all those silver strings."

"Icicles," Ellen nodded. "But …" Laughter formed in her throat as she squeezed Ruthie tightly. "I didn't know you went shopping!"

"Oh, I forgot." Ruthie scooted off her lap. "I wasn't 'spose to tell. It's a surprise."

"Ruthie," Bitty called from downstairs. "You want to lick this spoon?"

"It's all right if you want to go," Ruthie said. "I'll be busy. We are going to have cookies after we watch the 'Tivity."

"Thank you for your permission."

"It's all right. Now you better hurry or you'll be late for work,"

Festive. That was how she felt. Festive, for the first time in such a long time, she couldn't remember when. The streets were filled with cars going every direction. The mall was beautifully lit by all the seasonal lights. She paused, after parking the car, to appreciate the true meaning of Christmas. It really wasn't the shopping or the gifts, but the sweet spirit one felt inside when the world was right. Anne was recovering from the fright she had experienced. Bitty and Harriet were getting along, and though her house was full, possibly because it was the Holy season, all was well. She locked the car, forgetting any apprehension. She realized in her black dress and high heels she was dressed as so many others who were doing last minute shopping before heading off to celebrate.

Pressing through the crowd, she found Jenny finishing a sale.

"Wow! Aren't you the knockout?" Jenny stepped around her, admiring Ellen's wardrobe. "Two hours work for all that?"

Blushing, Ellen laid the tip of one finger on the tip of Jenny's nose. "I have a date."

"Touch you." Jenny replied, eyebrows raised, indicating immense curiosity. "And who is the lucky fellow?" She backed away, studying Ellen. "You're not telling, are you?"

"You wouldn't know him."

"Try me. I'd like to."

Mr. Shumacher approached, squelching their banter. "Um, Mrs. Anderson, I see you will be here a short time."

The two young women grinned at each other. "That means get to work." Jenny quipped. "Another day older and deeper in debt," she sang. "Two hours ain't nothing."

"Actually," Mr. Shumacher coughed, and said, "I think Ellen looks rather splendid." Seeming almost embarrassed, he made his escape to the office.

"He called you Ellen." Jenny rolled her eyes. "I guess the way to a man's heart isn't through his stomach, but his eyes, because," she grinned, "you do look splendid, my dear." Jenny skulked around the nearest aisle, bending to speak to a little boy who was sitting in one of the chair groupings waiting on his mother.

"How about another pair of shoes, Mrs. Jenkins? No? You're deciding? Just take your time." She tousled the boy's hair and came back to Ellen. "Old Shu is still anguishing over Jason. Almost to the point of not hiring another person, and it's Christmas coming right our way." Jenny shook her head, staring out into the mall. "Hello, Santa Claus, Merry Christmas, everyone wanting a special pair of boots. You know what I mean." Jenny wagged a finger in Ellen's face.

Mentally, Ellen crossed her fingers. She might have to change from the heels if Shumacher made her stay past seven. How would she explain that to Daniel Gates? It was a problem she wouldn't face until she had to. Somehow, she suspected, Mr. Gates didn't have to worry over a measly two hours in a minimum paying job to make ends meet. But she did. There was a washer to think about, not to mention she had overspent the budget on Christmas gifts. Ruthie's were one thing, a necessity, but Bitty and Harriet deserved something too. And Anne. If the blue and gray silk scarf were still in accessories, it would look lovely on Anne ... and then there was

Andy. Still unclear as to Andrew allowing their child to spend this holiday with his mother was an issue.

The first hour sped by with a rush of customers. One group would leave and another appear. Tan suede boots were the year's fad, with swinging balls made of fur on the long strings that wound around the boot, and every girl between seven and eleven, it seemed, had asked for them. Doc Martens were in demand by teenage boys. "I don't care if I never see another boot," Jenny whispered in passing the last hour. Stopping suddenly, she leaned in closer. "Get a load of what's coming through the door."

Curious, Ellen started to turn, instantly forbidding herself to do so. She saw him, reflected in the oval mirror on the opposite wall, as she deliberately glanced away.

"Man. Oh, man." Jenny studied him covetously.

"Close your mouth," Ellen whispered. Somewhat flustered herself, she busily straightened a small sign.

Jenny was now tugging at her sleeve, staring up into Ellen's face. "That's him, isn't it?" Jenny's hands flew to her cheeks. "Why, you're blushing." She gave a high pitched laugh. "Girl. Go get him."

He was spectacular. Dressed in a dark charcoal suit, Daniel Gates outshined any man in the shop. It wasn't what he was wearing, but how he wore it. Ellen wasn't sure any man had ever looked that good. A small silver bar crossed the red tie. She knew there would be matching links on the white shirt cuffs.

"The shoes are priceless," Jenny whispered. "Get a load of the shine."

"I'm not looking," Ellen said between closed lips. "They're probably plain black shoes."

"Honey, there is nothing plain about that man." Jenny giggled. "If Mr. Shumacher wants you to stay, I'll take your place. Hmm. Here he comes."

"Mr. Shumacher?" A knot twisted in Ellen's stomach.

"No, toots. It's your man." Jenny clutched a hundred-dollar pair of tennis shoes to her chest. "Actually, Mr. Shumacher is heading him off."

Frustration mounted. "I can't stand this," Ellen whispered. "Please tell me I don't have to explain this to Mr. Shumacher, or him."

"Why, I'll do it for you, *sugah*." Jenny's southern drawl came straight out of *Gone with the Wind*. "You can think about this tomorrow. I know I will."

The clock chimed seven. Funny how she'd never noticed how loud it was before. Both men were moving forward. Mr. Shumacher's hand was on Daniel Gates's back as they came down the center aisle.

"Ellen." Mr. Shumacher cleared his throat. "I wasn't aware you and Daniel were acquainted." His glance moved to Jenny. "There's a young lady up front looking for those tan suedes," he said easily. "Ellen, I'll relieve you behind the counter."

Having gathered her black wool coat, Ellen laid it across her arm. Aware Jenny was dying to be introduced, she wondered how to get out of the shop with her dignity intact. In her present nervous state of mind, she knew Jenny would do something. She fidgeted with the small purse she had chosen for the night. She was not a school girl with a crush. She was a grown woman. That hadn't had a date in three years! She thought dating was a thing of the past. She would raise her daughter, get a nursing certificate, and live life as best she could, devoid of men. Jenny, ever curious, lingered while he helped Ellen into her coat.

"Ready?" Daniel took her hand, tucking it possessively inside his arm.

His eyes were on her and looked neither right nor left until he had her safely inside a shiny black Deville. "You look lovely," he said as they drove out of the parking lot.

"So do you." Her voice sounded faint in her own ears.

He laughed. "Thank God for that," he said, relieved. "I wasn't sure I passed the test." He drove the streets from memory. Short cuts to Main left off Williams and Thornton. Both streets, his mother told him when he was a child, were named after doctors. Medical center of the world, he'd understood then, and things hadn't changed. Located halfway between Memphis and St. Louis, people came from surrounding states. The new hotel should be thriving. He pulled the Deville into a VIP parking space, turned off the motor, and leaned toward Ellen. "Are you ready for this?"

"You didn't tell me where we are going. What is this, some kind of opening?"

"Exactly," he grinned, "before the highways and byways find we are here, and hopefully that won't be long. Grand opening is next week. This is a preview of things to come. Investors, city council men, and what have you, even the governor."

"I'm impressed." She glanced down at the full length coat with its fur collar and cuffs.

"You're fine," he said. His eyes were on her as he opened the door. "Perfect." Once he had her out of the car, they sprinted toward the hotel already lined with people. They entered through a side door bearing a private entrance sign. She'd say one thing: what he did, he did with boldness. If they threw him out, she would have to follow. He pressed on, through a private hall to a massive lobby filled with more people. She tried to get a glance at each woman, scrutinizing, however quickly, the way they were dressed. She wondered why they were waiting as they loitered behind huge pots of palm and ficus trees. Huge bouquets of flowers were everywhere, with small white cards dangling, she supposed from well-wishers. He kept a hold on her arm as he smiled and spoke, and she realized everyone seemed to know him, or at least who he was. They were in a smaller area of the lobby when he ducked behind a latticed wall that was profusely covered in vines. A young lady, dressed in black, reached out, asking if she could take their coats. Then, going through a secret passage, they were in some sort of ball room. "Truly, I feel like 'Alice in Wonderland,'" she whispered.

"Take a deep breath," he said, enjoying what he was seeing on her face.

"Those chandeliers," she whispered. "Just one must cost more than I make in a year."

"This is Hutson Hall at its finest," he agreed. "Glad you approve."

"Someone with really good taste built this," she said, "and very wealthy, I imagine."

"You can say that again," he laughed. "For Hutson's sake, let's hope this is a very successful night." He squeezed her hand. "The press is here covering the grand opening, and it has been my experience the write-up can make or break a business."

For a moment, Ellen sensed his body tense. "What's wrong?"

"Nothing, really," he replied, but there was a glimmer of something Ellen could not decipher in his eyes. "I just saw an acquaintance across the room, sad to say, I had hoped would not be here."

She felt the pressure on her hand as he led through aisle after aisle of white-clothed tables, centered by clear vases holding red roses. The waiters seemed to glide quietly from table to table, whispering and receiving orders as the guests circled the room finding acquaintances. Ellen almost stalled, mesmerized by the sheer beauty of the room, the dresses the women were wearing, and the elegance of the men in their dark suits and tuxedos. She thought he spoke as she glanced away from the people to see him smiling down on her. "I'm sorry," she felt a blush washing over her face again.

"I was enjoying watching you, watching them." He squeezed her hand. "It's all right." There was a crinkle around his eyes. "Perhaps I should warn you, an old friend is here." He paused. "How do I say this? Madonna can be a bit of a barracuda. I thought we might avoid her, but I see she is tracking us."

"This friend," she hesitated. "How do I say this? Perhaps she is the one I felt you tense upon seeing her across the room?" To his nod, she said, "And this person was, perhaps, a girlfriend, or more?"

"Emphasis on the *perhaps* would be correct."

Ellen smiled. "I lay no claim on you. You are free to go."

"Who said I want to go?" He teased, bending to stare into her face, "Not that it matters, just thought I should warn you. And remember, I don't want to leave you." For a moment his eyes shone with warmth, bordering on intimacy, they both recognized. She had only a moment to relish the thought when they were interrupted by a swishing sound and the appearance of a breathtaking beautiful woman. Clothed in a ruby red skirt, with a low cut velvet top revealing more flesh than necessary, Ellen met Daniel's friend. A swish of taffeta brushed close to Daniel's pant leg; a diamond-ensconced hand claimed his as Madonna stepped between them.

"Daniel, darling," a throaty voice spoke into his ear, ice and velvet dripping of times past and times anticipated. "Lord knows I was just waiting for your arrival. I haven't seen you in ages."

"It has been years," Daniel replied dryly. "How are you, Madonna?"

"Much better, darling, now that you are here." She examined Ellen, as one might study an abstract drawing.

"You will excuse us, won't you? Daniel and I are old friends."

"Madonna, meet Ellen." Behind Madonna's back, he winked at Ellen. "My best friend."

"You must be new in town," Madonna said. "I don't believe I've seen you around."

"Then you do not frequent the mall," Ellen replied. "I work there."

Daniel decided Ellen could hold her own. Leaning back on his heels, he listened. Here was fire and ice. Calm and chaos. While he knew very little about Ellen, Madonna usually laid a path of destruction, caring little who she destroyed as long as she had her way. His was a firsthand experience. Madonna shrugged, negatively. "Anyone who is anyone does not go there these days."

Before Ellen could reply, Daniel tucked her arm possessively beneath his, starting to move away. "Nice seeing you, Madonna," he grinned, "but we need to work the crowd."

Ellen would have sworn Madonna was sulking, as she replied, "But Daniel, I want us to get together."

"Jake might not like that, Madonna. Remember. You are married."

"No." She stomped her foot, seemingly amazed at her own action. "I am not."

"Well, that was invigorating, wasn't it?" Daniel grinned, his arm drawing Ellen closer to his side. "Come with me, little Alice, and I will show you the rest of Hutson Hall. There are no more hidden passages, but if it is a tea party you desire, we can do that."

"I don't think these people are drinking tea," she said, raising an eyebrow.

"No, probably not." He hesitated, "Are you against dancing?"

"No."

His smile was infectious.

"I may be a woman of faith, but I used to attend an exercise class that was more dance than knee bends and leg lifts."

"And you liked it?"

"The best exercise I could find: a bunch of women dancing solo, and most of us were pregnant."

His laughter filled the room. "I bet that was fun to watch. So shall we?" He led her into the second ball room, where a full band was playing an old Glenn Miller song. "I think that is what Aunt Georgia calls a song to jitter bug to, but that is not my forte. Shall we do a fast two-step?" He held out his hands and she accepted.

"I'm a bit rusty," she said.

She was thankful the dance was a fun two-step that bordered on a bit of swing and waltz. They found they had a rhythm all their own, nothing embarrassing or intimidating.

"Me thinks the lady had more than an exercise class; there's some real movement in those bones." He tapped his forehead with one finger. "Confession time."

"My mother thought the quality of my life would be enhanced by piano and dance lessons." She returned his smile as the band began a new number.

"It is good to know I figured that out." He stepped back, placing one hand on her shoulder, the other on the small of her back. "One look at her and I said, she's the one." He sang as they danced. Grinning, he whirled her around. "I've forgotten the exact words." He did not tell her he was making up the lyrics. "I couldn't sleep, my heart had come undone. It's not just the way she looks, it's not just the way I feel … it's a matter of life going on. " All around them, people were clapping as they finished the dance, and a member of the band came with a microphone to pin on his lapel.

"Good to see you, Daniel," the young man said, patting his back. "We've had a request. Here you go; scan these pages and see if you can do it like you used to." To Ellen, he confided. "This boy's past is catching up with him, except now he sings in churches."

"You have got to be kidding." He stared at the back of the musician as he hurried to join the band. The first notes sounded lonely and lingered while Daniel studied the music. "My lady," he said, leading her to the first empty table, "I shall return."

The band began to the good-natured clapping of the dancers and those gathered around the edge of the dance floor. He began, faking wiping sweat from his brow, to immerse himself in the lyrics of the song. As he neared the end, he came, dropping to one knee to sing to Ellen, taking her right hand and placing a kiss on her fingertips, and then rising to bow profusely before the crowd that was whistling and clapping loudly.

"I have to have fresh air after that," he said. "Here, take my jacket and let's step out on the veranda."

"You are just full of surprises," she said. "Dancing and singing."

"Yeah, Aunt Georgia put me through the paces too. No dance lessons." He grinned. "She taught me those moves just in time for high school dances. She didn't believe in wallflowers."

"Voice lessons?" she asked. "I suppose you play the piano too?"

"He's a pretty well-rounded man," Madonna said, stepping out of the shadows, her hand sliding down Daniel's shirt sleeve. "I knew you would come out here. Like old times." She turned to Ellen. "There's little I don't know about Daniel."

While Ellen did not believe people lived previous lives, she was certain Madonna would have been a cat, the way she purred and stretched her tendons.

CHAPTER 6

That was the first evening Ellen accompanied Daniel. She could only wonder at the number of people who seemed to know him and invited him to holiday gatherings. And she was amazed that her small daughter and Bitty had so many plans to attend to since Bitty started spending nights at their home. When she prayed, she wondered why God was allowing her to spend time with Daniel Gates, knowing when he returned to his home there would be a great void, for she truly enjoyed being with him.

Then there was Madonna, wearing beautiful clothes on her toned and tanned body, appearing as out of a vapor by Daniel's side whispering words Ellen partly heard and otherwise imagined ... remembrance of times past, occasional shared laughter, and then Madonna slithering away as Ellen felt Daniel's demeanor change: his body temporarily stiffening as though he were quenching hidden anger, a frown clouding his features.

These were the warning signs Ellen registered and thought on the next day, wondering why the mere sight of his arrival at the shoe shop made her heart sing, when she knew this happiness was only temporary.

"Lord, protect my heart," she prayed. "Am I to end this relationship of friendship because I will be hurt? Is there a reason you are allowing it?" she asked.

The days were passing, and though she feared hurt, she found herself humming, looking forward to each date. Daniel Gates was an honorable man. He treated her with respect. He did not press his friends on her, but he did introduce her to them.

Madonna came into the powder room, watching as Ellen dried her hands and prepared to leave. "You know," she said, "it's only a matter of time until Daniel comes back to me."

Staring at their reflections in the mirror, Ellen sighed. "I guess that is Daniel's choice." She left, the door swinging shut on Madonna's laughter.

Returning to Daniel's side, neither his quiet mood nor Madonna's joining them surprised her as Madonna's hands on Daniel left no doubt she was asserting ownership. In Ellen's mind, she assumed this was God's answer to her prayer and the many questions. She tried distancing herself to allow them time together. When asked by their hostess to play the piano, she was glad for the distraction and the group that gathered around to sing.

Driving home, there was an unbearable silence, unlike any they had shared before.

"Ellen," he said. "Did I do something to displease you?"

"Strange you should ask," she replied. "I was wondering the same. But then I thought it over. You and Madonna have a history. We don't." She knew she sounded harpy. "I really think the two of you should relieve me of this cute little threesome and get on with your already forged alliance." She had forgotten how ill-willed words sounded when two people disagreed, until now, but she continued. "I have this sweet little daughter I can spend time with." She tried to smile sweetly. "It's all right."

"Alliance?" His brows knit dangerously together. "An alliance? We are not a country, negotiating, if that is what you think." He turned to her. "Does this have anything to do with Madonna? I saw her follow you. And then she came out, all over me. I guess I thought you would do something. Help me out."

"Me? Help you out. I distanced myself for the two of you."

"Why?" He seemed genuinely puzzled. "I suppose you have heard still waters run deep?" He pulled into an empty parking lot, pushed the gear into place, and turned to stare her direction. "Madonna dumped me, years ago, when we were engaged, to marry my best friend. I lost two friends at the same time. And it has taken a long time to forget the pain." He sighed, a dragged breath. "Until you ..."

"Oh." The truth dawned. She hadn't realized Madonna was the one. She should have. She bowed her head as the tears pooled. "Then I can imagine your pain. My Madonna was named Jeff."

"I've been very careful," he said slowly. "Since then, I have not even fathomed interest in another woman, so great was the humiliation I felt Madonna and my friend had caused me. It was like a scratchy garment on a thirty-year-old man that had to be removed again and again. Aunt Georgia tried to say the shame was not mine to bear, and I suppose I worked through that because it no longer bothers me."

"You are still in love with her?"

The puzzled expression dawned in his troubled eyes.

"You don't have to explain," she said. "Two weeks ago we were strangers." She sighed. "Frankly, this is a bit too much for me. I don't belong in your crowd. I don't have the clothes, the money, nor really the time to give away with my schedule of work and school and my darling little girl."

Ellen felt pressured, intimidation attacking her, belligerent now that her emotions had surfaced and a last minute need to explain herself. This other woman had such a hold on him; she was only someone to accompany him to social gatherings. "What I am trying to say, I have a precious little girl I need to put to bed each night, and," her voice struggled, as she was near tears, "I think I realized, for the umpteenth time tonight, I don't fit in and I probably never would." She brushed away the tears. "And I'm sorry I'm crying, I really don't know why I am, because we have no strings attached. You are not like Jeffrey. You have been kind and attentive, but I realize I am only someone you invite to attend parties with and we aren't fighting, it's just that ... I really don't know what it is."

She gathered the small purse to her chest and reached for the door handle. "I'll catch a cab. It's the sensible thing to do." Fumbling, she opened the door to get out.

His hand was on her shoulder. "I'm not in love with Madonna. That was over a long ago. I've had a hard time even wanting to trust a woman again." His hand tightened on hers. "Come back in. Don't think of a cab. Let me take you home." He was peering into her eyes as if demanding she pay attention. "I never intended to trust another woman," he said softly, "until I happened into Shumacher's shop." He grinned. "I seemed to have no control over anything." His eyes warmed, and the gloominess of the evening was replaced with a smile. "Just answer one question, Ellen Anderson. Are you interested in me at all?"

"I thought you and Madonna wanted to be together. She implied you and she had a history, but no one told me she was the one."

"Loyalty among friends," he sighed. "Good or bad. They wouldn't."

His fingers were rubbing the tips of her fingernails. "Will you continue to see me, meet my aunt, and just take things slow? No more worries over Madonna, now you know the story." Tilting her head toward him, he kissed the top of her head and the tip of her nose, and then his lips settled on hers, a searching, questioning kiss that promised more as he pulled her into his arms, smelling the fragrance of her hair, knowing it would be like this ... the softness of her, their yielding oneness as the rhythm of her breathing settled and the tension left her body. "No pressure, just more good times," he whispered into her ear. "Aunt Georgia wants to meet you, and I want to meet your little daughter. I want to do this right."

She went to bed troubled. Perhaps she was in over her head. Daniel Gates had popped into her life at an unexpected time. True, tonight she had misread the situation. Hadn't she learned, all it takes to upset a woman is another woman? Jeffrey's unfaithfulness had left her cautious, until Daniel Gates showed up at Shumacher's needing boots. She turned, twisting the covers. She must move slowly. Any woman would feel pampered walking beside a handsome man who showered her with praise and was pleased with her appearance, happy to introduce her to his friends, attentive, and kind. She sighed. Now he wanted her to meet his aunt? She should break it off, but she couldn't. She was drawn to Daniel Gates.

Trying to think new thoughts, she stretched her toes to the end of the covers as Ruthie rolled close. Anne was asleep in the next room, Bitty upstairs in her attic. A pile of clothes folded by the door reminded her: the washer must be working again. The house was quiet except for the squeaks and groans of aging. Her mind roamed, remembering only by the grace of God there was a roof over their heads. When her grandmother died, there was an inheritance, enough to buy the old house on the hill and to help with the expense of a sitter for Ruthie while she went to nursing school. Finances were tight to bare existence, but they were blessed. *Thank you, God, for Bitty taking care of Ruthie*, she whispered, kissing the back of Ruthie's head.

Finally drifting off to sleep, with Ruthie snuggled to her side, in her dreams Ellen saw Daniel. He walked with assurance, leaned toward her, and kissed the top of her head, his eyes mellowing with liquid warmth that drew her in, making her feel protected in a way she had not known. For a moment she awakened … it seemed so real. And tonight she was ready to end that blessed feeling. *Oh, Lord, heavenly Father,* she prayed, *help me with this. I need your guidance. I've failed once, so miserably, I cannot do that again.*

"I see the washer is miraculously working again," she said next morning.

Bitty smiled. "That would be Harriet's repairman. She sent him over after he fixed her furnace. Who knew? He works down at the appliance shop that sells about anything you want, so he said." Her smile widened. "And Harriet paid. Said it was the least she could do since you took her in." Bitty poured a second cup of coffee and motioned for Ellen to sit a minute. "You got time to drop off a package for me? I want to send my brother's grandbabies something for Christmas."

"Sure. I don't know how you do what you do, Beatrice." Ellen slid across the chair, arms on the table. "May the good Lord help us if ever a man takes a liking to you. You would make him a wonderful wife, but I don't know what would happen to Ruthie and me." She studied Bitty in earnest. "Do you ever tire, taking care of all you do for us?"

"No." Bitty's lips pressed firmly together, her eyes narrowing as she thought. "It seems like I came back to life. For a while, after Larry died, I lost track of time. One day followed another, all just alike. Grieving is hard business, and I wasn't good at it."

"But you can't tie your life up taking care of us. You will have to move on, and I dread when that day comes." Ellen drained the cup, standing to take it to the sink. She returned to Bitty, kissing her cheek. "Have I said *thank you* lately?"

"You don't have to." Bitty replied, her voice ginger-snap firm. "Besides, the day hasn't arrived for me to leave you and Ruthie. As she says, we still have lots to learn."

"A PENNY FOR YOUR THOUGHTS." Already she recognized his voice as she glanced around to see if Mr. Shumacher was present, and then to where Daniel stood smiling at her. "He is down the hall visiting his friend," Daniel said.

"What brings you out so early?"

"You." He handed the three remaining boxes, one at a time, for her to place on the shelf. "I wanted to be sure we didn't end last night on a bad note." He waited for her reply. "No regrets?" he questioned. "None on my part."

He knew she would spend most of the morning pondering what to do, with no answer in mind. "You were in deep thought. I stood here watching you a few minutes."

"I was thinking," she nodded.

"Hmmm. That can be dangerous." A thread of humor was in his voice, "And the answer is? Whether to continue seeing the tall dark stranger, or ban him completely from your life." He sank dramatically to one knee, clutching her hand. "Please, Miss Ellen, don't turn me away. I need you to rescue me one more time. I won't make any demands, and I promise I'll be good."

Laughter spilled out of Ellen. "Get up. Get up." She pulled against his weight. "What would the customers think, or Mr. Shumacher? I would be so embarrassed." Closing her eyes, she wondered how he could mangle her decision so quickly. Without his presence she could think for her sake and Ruthie's she must stop seeing Daniel, but when he was near she wavered, in fact could hardly bear the thought.

"Before I do get up." He remained on his knee, regardless that she tugged. "I have one thing to tell you. I do not love Madonna.

Any frustration on my part upon seeing Madonna follow you into the powder room last night should be forgotten, and this is important ... amazing, profoundly amazing ... I feel I have already started trusting women again. Otherwise," he grinned, rising, "I would not be here." He stood, smiling down into her eyes. "Well, that's two things, isn't it?"

Arriving as Daniel left, Jenny had questions. "Hey, girl. From the hall, I saw your man on his knee. Was that a marriage proposal? Although I'd say that is a bit fast. How do you feel about him?"

"When I'm with him, I'm happy. He is so gentle and kind and funny. But, last night I was almost one hundred percent sure I should end it." She sought Jenny's understanding. "Please realize this ... he asked me out to be his escort at social functions."

"Girl." Jenny shook her head, curls bouncing up and down. "That was in the beginning. I see real chemistry between you two."

"Still, I'm not sure I could ever fit into his world. No," she said, "I think I should quit this whole deal. No more meeting his friends and especially his family."

"You have got to be out of your mind," Jenny exclaimed. "Quit seeing Mr. Tall, Dark, and Handsome, what's his name?" She stared at Ellen as if she thought her crazy. "Girl, these opportunities don't come around often." Dramatically Jenny swept one arm around the room. "Do you see anyone else lining up offering themselves? Where is my knight in silver armor, copper, tin, aluminum foil even, for that matter?"

She wasn't finished. "Ellen, you work all the time. Either you are studying or here for old Shu, or at your boarding house full of desperate women, not to mention your quest for knowledge to serve the medical world as Florence Nightingale." She sighed. "Mr. Handsome will retire from sight, once the holidays are over, to his abode in California. All the glamour will disappear with his dashing face gone, and we will return to our dismal little lives of daily toil. "Girl," she shouted, poking Ellen in the rib. "Let him stay this short while. I like looking at him."

Jenny came to rest, one arm draped over a rise of shoe boxes, the other angled at her hip as she stared into Ellen's eyes. "Can he stay? Mr. Candy for the Eyes?"

"I am praying about it," Ellen replied, relieved to see a customer come into the shop.

"Pray?" Jenny flounced away. "Pray? What are you, the Virgin Mary?"

Silently the thoughts drifted through Ellen's mind. Yes, she would pray more. Evidently God had meant for her to meet Daniel Gates or he would never have put him in her path, but did God have an ulterior plan. Bringing her mind back to business, classes were ending for holiday break and Mr. Shumacher had asked her to work more hours. She could use the hours. The old furnace seemed to be hiccupping along these days. She never knew what was next. And her baby was turning into one long-legged little girl. Ruthie had needs. Yes, she would pray. That was what she had to do. God was the heavenly Father that got her through life.

Sometimes she was so tired, and this weekend was no different. The ladies were planning to attend Christ Church, all for Ruthie. Did not Scripture say a little child shall lead them? Maybe God had an answer waiting for all her questions

Still, when Daniel's call came through, her heart lightened. "I waited until Shu left," he said. "Are we still on? You wouldn't let me down, would you? Remember? I want you to meet my aunt. She wants to meet you."

CHAPTER 7

Candles gleamed in each window. Christ Church was aglow. Greenery hung in swags along the ceiling rafters. Everywhere there was greenery, tiny white lights twinkled, bringing one's eyes to the celestial view of blue sky through the glass dome. Another denomination might have a glass cathedral, but Christ Church had a dome. People traveled miles to worship in Christ Church and peer into heaven's skies.

"Oh. Oh," Ruthie gaped at the nativity scene on the raised platform that held the pulpit and behind it the choir loft. "Oh, Mommy, it's baby Jesus."

"The Nativity certainly looks real," Mrs. Becker whispered.

"I want to hold the baby Jesus."

"Sweetums, no one can hold the baby Jesus. Now let's sit down and be quiet."

Mrs. Becker was leading the entourage down the aisle in search of a pew with room for all. Nodding importantly at first one and then another, she finally stopped in the third aisle from the front, waiting for Ellen to enter, then Ruthie, and next Bitty.

"Mommy, he's so beautiful." Ruthie turned to look at Bitty. "Isn't he beautiful? I want to hold him. I won't hurt him, will I, Bitty?"

Bitty pressed a kiss on Ruthie's forehead. "Yes, he is beautiful, and no you won't hurt him, but what if everyone wanted to hold him and the church worship hour would never begin?"

"But Bitty, isn't it more important to hold baby Jesus?"

"Shh." Ellen laid a finger to her lips. "Ruthie, let Anne in the pew." Anne pressed in between Bitty and Mrs. Becker, holding Andy on her lap. Andrew had allowed her time with their son, knowing Christmas Day this year belonged to him. Anne's expression mirrored the anticipation of the group. This was a very special day.

"Good morning." A robed gentleman bustled up the steps to stand behind the podium. "Welcome. Welcome. Christ Church welcomes you to join in praise and worship this wonderfully crisp winter day as we all stand to sing." Organ notes soared throughout the sanctuary and voices rose, "Oh come let us adore Him, Christ the Lord."

Ruthie was practically bouncing up and down in excitement. When the choir pressed on into "Away in a Manger," she clapped her hands, leaning into Bitty's side. "Sing, Bitty, Jesus wants us to sing."

Ellen noticed Bitty sang "Away in the Manger" holding Ruthie's hand as if she drew strength from the child, but Mrs. Becker carried each song with a robust soprano, patting Anne occasionally on the arm as if to say, "Everything is all right."

The singing came to an end. The pastor rose to stand before them.

"It's him. It's him," Ruthie whispered loudly, clasping Ellen's neck. "While Dora rests. He says, 'Welcome to Christ Church.'"

Embarrassed, Ellen tried to quiet Ruthie. To her relief, a lady sitting in the pew behind leaned forward whispering, "She's right. I have a little girl too, who watches Dora every day. The pastor does come after Dora."

The congregation quieted. "As we enter this wonderful sacred time of year," he began, "we have much for which we are thankful." He peered at the Christ Church people, speaking as one would to dear friends. "All who entered the doors today may not feel the joy of the season. Perhaps there are among us heartache, disappointment, and wounded spirits. It is to you I speak. Today as we begin our journey toward the story of Jesus' birth, let us remember words our Savior gave to us while He was on this earth. Please turn in your Bibles to John 14:1. 'Let not your hearts be troubled.' Yes, you believe in Him, or you are searching whether to believe in Him, or you would not be here. Jesus said, 'Let not your hearts be troubled.'

"I watched the expressions on your faces as we were singing. And while I will not divulge exactly who I was watching, I saw a little girl singing with such passion, seeming to know the words to each Christmas hymn, and oh, the joy and enthusiasm could not be missed. Jesus said, 'Let not your hearts be troubled.' He also said we are to come to Him with the innocence of a child, trusting, relying upon Him with the heart of a child. Not seared over, denying His great love, but putting away heartaches made from hurt. Perhaps we have been denied, rejected, abandoned, and disappointed by others' actions. We are not alone. Has anyone suffered more than our Savior suffered?

"It is appropriate we begin our first Sunday remembering the little baby born of virgin birth would be rejected, humiliated, scorned, and abused, all in order for us to have the comfort of His love, the peace that comes to hearts even in the worst of times, all because God sent His Son to earth for us that we might be saved. As we think of our own hurt, the humiliation, rejection, and abuse heaped on our lives due to others' actions," he paused, waiting to let the last words sink in, "let us think also about the hope we have, the knowledge that God watches over us. Even in the worst hour of our life, He brings peace and comfort. How does He do that? Let us turn to Scripture. Even a murderer, a thief, the one who betrayed Jesus, found hope."

"I'd say," a man in front said aloud, "that pretty much covers everyone here."

Ellen happened to glance down the pew, seeing Harriet blanch while Anne was twisting her hands until they were red. Bitty remained stoic. Inwardly, Ellen sighed.

A quiet spell had overtaken them as they filed one by one down the aisle, shook hands with the pastor, and nodded to those who pressed forward to speak as they hurried to Anne's larger vehicle. Seat belts fastened, Andrew in his seat, the group headed to Harriet's home for Sunday dinner. No one broke the silence. By some greater power, it seemed all were drawn into personal private thought. Ruthie and Andy were asleep in minutes while Anne drove.

"Aren't we the quiet ones," Harriet remarked as they arrived. "Come, now. I made a roast with all the trimmings, and the table is set, except for the napkins."

"Let me help you," Bitty offered. "Too many in a kitchen get in each other's way."

Ellen poured tea in the glasses as Anne placed white napkins next to the silverware.

"Her home is beautiful," Anne whispered. "Mr. Becker must have served her well." Glancing around, she continued, "It's a grand old lady, as you say about your house, Ellen."

"But this grand old lady has all the fixings," Ellen nodded. "Mine could use a fix."

Once they were seated at the table, Harriet looked to Ellen. "I know you pray dear; I heard you many times when I was sleeping on your sofa. Do you mind?"

"Lord, we thank you for the beautiful sermon we have shared today and for this dinner Mrs. Becker has prepared. We ask you now to bless this food she offers in the name of friendship; bless it to our bodies and our bodies to your service. In your precious name. Amen."

"What's servon?" Ruthie asked as she came to the table from sleeping on Mrs. Becker's bed, and where Andy remained oblivious to anything else at the moment. Rubbing her eyes, she climbed onto the chair beside Ellen. "What's servon?"

"*Sermon*, Sweetums," Ellen spooned mashed potatoes onto her daughter's plate. "Sermon means the words and Scripture from the Bible the pastor read."

"How can we serve?" Suppressing a yawn, Ruthie forked a green bean. "I want to serve Jesus. How can I?"

"May I tell you later, Sweetums?"

"Please." Anne's lovely haunted eyes lifted to Ellen's. "I want to hear too."

"I'll do my best, but I'm not the best example. This last year I've failed miserably." Fork midair, she began. "Serving Jesus is when we commit ourselves to live right before others, help those in need, and when the Spirit leads, tell them about Jesus' love."

"Isn't that too easy?" Mrs. Becker asked. "I know you do that, Ellen, but there has to be more." She sighed. "I did attend church when I was a child, but all that fell aside in the busyness of life." Glancing around the room, she continued, "With career and marriage, it seemed there wasn't enough time to give up the weekends for church."

"Two, possibly three hours a week?" Ellen questioned softly. "I know. I'm guilty. I told myself it was my schedule, the classes, work, and study, but today's sermon has made me think." She paused to take in each one of them, her eyes resting on Anne seated across the table, "I think the benefits of God's Word far outweigh my busy schedule. I need to hear God's Word. It will soften the hardness I encounter everywhere I go."

"Tell me what you mean, *when the Spirit leads*," Anne said. "I am embarrassed to ask, but I didn't have much raising in a church. My mother was always subdued by the alcohol, and my stepfather did the best he could, working and caring for all." Lapsing in memory, Anne's voice became almost inaudible, "But I just don't know about Jesus or the Spirit's leading."

Folding her hands in her lap, Ellen searched for words to explain. Here, around this table sat the people who had become most important in her life, a network of women with skills and willingness to help each other. "Do you know about salvation?" she asked.

"No," Anne sighed. "I hear the word, but it's foreign to me."

"At some time in life, a person becomes aware of Jesus." Ellen fixed her gaze on Ruthie. "Maybe they hear the story of his birth at Christmas, or at Easter, that he died on the cross. The wonderful saving part of his death for our sins is that he arose on the third day. It makes a person begin to wonder. If you are brought up in a Christian home, you understand Jesus' life easier, perhaps because it isn't all pressed on you at once."

"I've always heard the story," Anne replied. "Most everyone celebrates Christmas and Easter, whether they are Christian or not, but I've not heard much about salvation or the Spirit … I just had no one to ask. I've not really had anyone I trusted to tell me." She sighed. "But yes, once you hear the story, you do wonder."

Ruthie was busy chasing green beans across her plate with a fork. Ellen had an idea there would be a score of questions later; still, she decided, Anne needed to hear.

"You know Jesus was born a lowly birth, but he was sent to this earth by His heavenly Father to die for our sins that we might have eternal life, if we believe."

"That's a bit much, isn't it, Ellen?" A troubled expression was on Harriet's face. "How do we know that's true? What if it is another fairy tale?"

"Fairy tales don't convict you, do they?" Ellen smiled. "You read them, they satisfy your urge for entertainment, but do they really speak to your heart?"

"Sometimes," Harriet grinned. "But go on."

"When Jesus died on the cross, in time the Holy Spirit came. Had Jesus not died for us, the Holy Spirit would not have come. It is the work of the Holy Spirit to speak to our hearts, convicting us of the sin in our life and our need to ask for forgiveness. You remember the pastor read the Scripture; Jesus said if I go away, I will send the comforter? That is the Holy Spirit, who also joins us in our prayers to the Father. That's what it means when it says the Holy Spirit will do unction for us. But first we have to believe."

"I need to believe," Anne's soft voice trembled. "There's so much unrest in my life, sometimes I actually can't eat or sleep. Lately, it's been terrible."

"I believe," Ruthie piped up, "and I need unction. He could help me be good."

Laughter spilled out around the table. Harriet rose. "On that, Ruthie, we'll have dessert."

ELLEN LAID RUTHIE IN THE bed, pulled the covers up to her shoulders, and straightened her hair on the pillow. The child was dead tired, unused to a day of church and dinner at Mrs. Becker's, or having Andy to play with all evening. Anne had taken the little boy, not much older than a toddler, back to his father, to return more subdued and strained than before. While Ellen's own life was hectic, to say the least, rushing from one place to another, she worried over Anne. Anne had lost a few more pounds, evident by the way her clothes hung on her shoulders; even Mrs. McCallister, the nursing instructor had noticed. The problem with Andy's father was wearing thin, sometimes causing Anne's emotions to become visible to those who knew her, often spilling over into tears. At least Ellen did not have that concern. Jeff could care less about Ruthie's welfare; thus he was out of their life.

If it were true, as Bitty thought, that Anne wished to reunite with Andrew, then that would be enough to understand Anne seeming to be losing her way. But, if it were true Andrew abused Anne, why then, Ellen wondered, would Anne want to go back to that marriage?

Tiptoeing out of the room, Ellen went to her own, closing the door quietly. Thankful to have her own private bath, she turned the tap to fill the old claw-foot tub with water. She wanted to sink down into the sudsy bubbles Bitty had given her on her birthday and think as she soaked. She could only wonder if she had correctly answered Anne's questions during lunch. And Bitty had turned quiet, listening, but seeming to have no interest in the conversation. Still, Mrs. Becker was the most startling of all, comparing Jesus and salvation to a fairy tale.

Alone, with her mind questioning so many things, Ellen was suddenly aware her own heart was not as pure as it should be. Didn't she sometimes wish Jeffrey Anderson had to go through one-tenth the trials she suffered? Hadn't she allowed a faithless husband to come between her and her own well-meaning parents, who had known the truth about Jeffrey all along that he was philandering around sleeping with other women? While Jeffrey worked hard at persuading Ellen, her parents would never have plotted against him telling her lies, except they had never truly liked him. And he was a faithful, hardworking husband. He insisted she would have to choose: him or her parents. She had chosen Jeffrey, to one day find him in bed with another woman a few years younger than she and much prettier. Ellen sighed, so caught up in her own thoughts.

Forgiveness must come to all, she surmised, and it had to happen within one's own heart, whether one experienced a wandering or abusive husband or a worse fate, though at the time her own struggle felt profound. As for Harriet and Bitty, she could not allow herself to wonder what lay in their hearts. What terrible thing could one person do against others that so hardened one's heart that they turned away from the Lord?

Realizing she was turning into a prune, Ellen drained the tub, dried her hair, and was crawling into bed when she heard a soft knock on the door.

"Ellen, are you awake?"

"Come on in."

Anne hesitated and then came into the room.

"Can't you sleep?"

"I keep thinking about what you and the minister said."

Ellen motioned for her to sit on the bed. "I'm such a mess, Ellen."

Anne's eyes filled with tears. "I feel like if I don't find some peace soon, I'm going to self-destruct." Hands to her forehead, Anne stared at the quilt on Ellen's bed. She knew it was some patchwork pattern with zig-zagging squares, much like her life … one would have to choose the path wisely. Her shoulders began to shake until the sobs came, racking her body.

"How can I help?" Ellen asked softly.

"You handle everything with such calm, Ellen, while I find myself falling apart when I leave Andy with his dad, when the car doesn't start, or I don't have money for gas, even when I come here."

"Oh, Anne, I'm anything but calm." What she saw in Anne was comparable to what she had felt when Jeffrey left. Misery claimed Anne as wholeheartedly as it had Ellen. "Why does coming here upset you?"

"I feel so guilty," Anne sobbed, "like I'm a freeloader sponging off you."

"Did you ever think, maybe the two of us together, might be stronger? What if we did not share this friendship?"

"You would still have Bitty. Oh, Ellen, I've made such a mess of my life."

"Well," Ellen smiled. "You cannot corner the market on that. I'm no great sage, but neither of us is very old. Unless, I miss my guess, what lies before us is far longer than what lays behind." She reached over to cup Anne's chin in her hand, "Enough of this … now what is it you don't understand about what I said? Maybe that is something I can clarify."

"You may not think you are calm," Anne hiccupped, giggling a bit beneath the sadness of her eyes, struggling to breathe deeper and explain. "But you are. You are always saying you will pray about this or that, and I know you do." She sighed. "When I try to pray, I think I am more or less begging or pleading with your God to let me have the things I want, while you seem to pray for what is needed. And," she caught her breathe, "according to the minister, this morning there's more to it. I'm not even sure God hears me." She searched Ellen's face. "Does God hear us, when we don't even truly know him?"

"Lady, you do not ask simple questions." Ellen rested her back against the headboard of the bed. "Hmm. Let me tell you what

I know, and you can go see the minister to find out what I don't know. How's that?"

"Oh no, I could never face a minister," Anne protested.

Ellen smiled. "I was very young when I felt a tug in my heart to know about Jesus." Anne's countenance fell. "My parents raised me in church, so to speak. It is not your fault that yours did not. All I am saying is it makes a difference if you hear something every day," *from the time I was born, no doubt,* she thought, *just as Ruthie has.* "All I know is one day I had to give Jesus my heart, and as soon as I did I felt better."

"How do you do that?"

Reaching for her Bible on the bedside table, Ellen said, "Come on, get comfortable, and I'll show you the Scripture any would-be believer must read." She thumbed through the New Testament. "But it's up to you whether you make the decision to believe in Jesus or not. I firmly believe God hears the sinner's prayer."

An hour later, Anne and Ellen had read Scripture and prayed together, and Anne was on her way to bed. "It's all so new to me," she said, "but maybe there's hope."

Yawning, Ellen turned out the light. "Think it through and listen. In the stillness of your heart, your soul, your mind, you will know."

Across town, Bitty lay in the darkness, listening to the rumble of the train as it lumbered its way to a distance unknown. She'd decided to return to the apartment, mostly to think in the silence of her own home. Maybe she shouldn't have attended church with the ladies. The emotions she was feeling bordered on resentment and rebellion. Hadn't God, described as the loving Father in the minister's sermon, taken Larry? What good had come from that? The stillborn child that Larry was buried beside ... was there supposed to be an answer to turn the sadness she had felt into gladness, a morsel of understanding, perhaps? The only thing she understood, tonight in this midnight hour, was she wasn't going back. Not for the promise of hearing about Jesus' life, nor the celebration of his birth. Wasn't that what the minister promised? To help those who did not believe know Jesus, and if they believed to visit once more the hope and promise only Jesus offered for eternal life.

Larry, in his last days, reminded Bitty again and again that he believed. "I thought you did, too, Hon," he'd say. "Don't tell me a loving God wouldn't take me. Some things happen in life that we will never understand until Jesus explains them. That's when we get to heaven, Bitty. You have got to believe, God will get you through this." Even in his weakened state, Larry would say, "Trust in the Lord, Bitty. He will help you through every trial." Tears in his eye, Larry repeated, "I want to see you in heaven, Bitty. I'll be there waiting. I love you, hon."

His words were little comfort in the months following his death. The company Larry worked for went bankrupt, any stock they owned worthless, no safeguard for her future. Her bed was empty; she was cold. Bitty took a second job. Within the year she was informed Larry had invested, unbeknownst to her, in another stock, which was doing quite well, but by then, working had set a pattern that filled the lonely hours of her day.

She shared very little with others until Jeffrey Anderson asked her to clean the homes he built when his construction crews finished, and she met his wife, Ellen. At first she tried remaining aloof and unsociable toward Ellen, but that didn't work. Ellen's sincere interest in Bitty crumbled the wall bit by bit, and when Ruthie came along, Bitty was bought. Not by money, nor kind words, but by the winsome innocence of a little baby that grew into a little girl who gave back tenfold the love she received.

"I'm not going back," Bitty muttered, eyeing the clock on the dresser as she tossed and turned in the bed. "It doesn't matter if Anne and Harriet agree too. I won't." It broke her heart that Ruthie's expectant little face popped into her thoughts. Lord, how she loved that little girl, and she would never do anything to hurt her.

"Why ever did I agree to go?" Bitty stared through the darkness, the crack in the ceiling a reminder that dawn was drawing near, and she had to rise early to go back across town. "I should have let sleeping dogs lie," she whispered. "You hear me, Larry? I thought it was all settled."

Harriet Becker awakened early. The hands on the clock showed five, two hours earlier than she was accustomed to rising. There was little to fill her days. Without intending, she had enjoyed the days spent next door at Ellen's house. Certainly she never intended to let down her guard nor accept friendship. A smile flitted across her face ... that Ruthie could warm the heart of a murderer. God forbid. She had sat stone-faced most of the day, ignoring the squirmy little beast who had dragged every book she owned onto the sofa, and read in that high-pitched little voice word for word each book's story.

Finally the one called Bitty explained. "Memorized. She reads, some, but not that many words yet."

Even now, she could not believe she and Bitty would end up swapping recipes, even cooking together on Ellen's ancient stove. Whether her own furnace dying during a snow storm had been blessing or curse had been questionable. In the beginning she was certain it was a curse, but the laughter that spilled forth, spontaneously, in that house was contagious, and she realized most of it had to do with the child, which had become a blessing.

Yes. She missed them. There was more activity in one day in Ellen's house than a year in her own. She had actually prepared dinner for the group yesterday. That in its self was a miracle. She had not entertained in years. And it went well. Mentally she gave herself a pat on the back. But the conversation had taken a turn. Harriet climbed out of bed, drew on an old robe salvaged from the days when George Becker lived, and made her way to the kitchen.

She needed to sort yesterday's events over a cup of coffee. Yesterday was stuck in her mind. Anne seemed terribly troubled. Ellen dealt well with Anne. Bitty had withdrawn. Yes, Harriet noticed, Bitty had escaped into her own little shell, saying nothing, no clue as to how she felt about the minister's sermon. And what did I say? Chagrined, Harriet relived her own words; *I said it was a fairy tale.* Then why am I still dwelling on it, and why was it hard to go to sleep last night?

"If I thought there was the slightest hope I could be forgiven for my terrible secret, perhaps I would also believe," Harriet said aloud. But George said the past was the past, not to speak of it again, and no one need ever know. "Do I care if someone knows, now, after all these years of cutting myself off from others? Was it worth it?" She poured steaming coffee into a cup. "What has it got me? Now I'm talking to myself."

Taking a seat at the table by the kitchen window, Harriet glanced toward Ellen's house. Now why in the world was a ladder standing against the back of the house, and who was that walking toward an old van in the parking lot?

CHAPTER 8

Garcia French stumbled across the street. His legs felt like wooden blocks, and his hands were numb all the way up to his armpits. What was he going to tell the boss, and what was he going to tell Onie? He had told her he would only be gone a short while. Placing a hand over each ear, he wondered that his ears hadn't frozen off. "They should just fall off, *plink plink*," he muttered as he tried to open the van door. It wouldn't budge. Garcia brought one fist down on it, cursing under his breath. The handle fell on the street, landing with a thud in the snow. Garcia danced, one foot to the other. Agitated at his own stupidity, he clumped around to the other side, managed to open the door, and slid across the seats and under the steering wheel. "Glad I got gas this time," he said aloud. "Now if the old junker will crank a motor." He turned the key, listening as a ragged whir of the starter turned to a grind. The engine whined and caught.

Garcia's laughter reached a demonic pitch as he backed across the parking lot and headed home. No one needed to know he'd fallen asleep doing surveillance, nor that his intention to grab the little girl had failed again. No sir, no one's business. "Night time's the best time," he hummed, never once considering twice he'd failed, and the boss was growing tired of Garcia's bungling.

The phone rang. A voice asked, "You got the girl?" As he listened, sweat broke out on Garcia's brow, mindless of the frozen state of his body. "You know too much, French. You deliver, or we're going to have to take matters into our own hands. You will be our first project."

―▸ ◂―

DANIEL SAT IN HIS UNCLE'S chair gazing out the window as winter mix pelted the driveway. Somehow it was comforting to remember the years growing up under his aunt and uncle's watchful eye. Now when he visited, Aunt Georgia insisted, "Sit in Bill's chair. He would want you to." She came into the room now.

"You seemed lost in thought. Want to share?"

"I wish Uncle Bill was still here. You must miss him very much."

"Yes, I do," she sighed. "The first year was the hardest." She glanced around the room. "No papers strewn across the floor, by his chair. There is no one to share that second cup of coffee." A wistful tone entered her voice. "He was a good man, tenderhearted and kind. I had hoped we would grow old together." She laughed, self-consciously. "Well, I know, to you I'm old, maybe I should say grow older together. But he's gone."

"Are people ever truly gone, Aunt Georgia? I will never forget Uncle Bill."

"No, I suppose not. They live on in our memory, don't they?"

"Yes, they do," he agreed, "some more than others."

She realized he was thinking of his own father. When Bill's sister, Elizabeth, married Dane Gates, the whole family had been up in arms, saying Dane Gates was not a marrying man. He played around too much. And they had been right, but, she thought, staring at Elizabeth and Dane's son, this one was more like his uncle than either parent. She supposed having no children of their own, she and Bill had doted on Daniel as if he were their own. *Of course Daniel must go to college. Of course we will fund his way.* Georgia laughed. She could hear Bill's voice in her head, even now.

"What's that about?" Daniel asked.

She grinned. "It was Bill's voice in my head," she replied, "telling me how proud of you he is."

"You both always wanted what was best for me. I can't tell you how humbling that is, and I appreciate every effort you made in raising me and encouraging me."

"You do tell me," she said softly. "You are the only child we ever had. I guess our hopes and dreams have always centered on you." For a moment, she hesitated. "Was there any reason in particular you didn't bring the young lady to meet me at the opening?"

Daniel laughed, rising to his feet. "I wondered when we would get around to that." Stepping across the room, he leaned down to give Georgia a hearty hug and then kissed the top of her hair. "Actually, I am saving her for a very special time. I don't want to scare her off. She's pretty cautious, I can tell you. I'm afraid she will bolt and run."

"Why's that, dear?"

"I would guess the husband dealt a pretty hard blow."

"She is divorced?"

"Yes, she is, with a little girl to raise all on her own." He sighed, "I think she's leery of men altogether. He must have hurt her pretty bad."

"And you can sympathize, because you also have been hurt?"

"Too say the least," he shrugged, returning to his uncle's chair. "Yeah."

"How was the encounter with Madonna?"

"I didn't know Madonna was divorced." There was a question hanging in the air.

"Really?" Georgia sighed. "Then it went through. I saw no need to tell you something I wasn't sure of. Her mother hasn't divulged that bit of information yet. I guess Madonna was her true self."

"Brash as ever," Daniel agreed. "Rude to Ellen." Again he shrugged powerful shoulders, straightening in the chair, to say, "It seems there's nothing new about Madonna. Why didn't you and Uncle Bill warn me, back then?"

"Some things you have to experience. Had we told you Madonna was just like her mother, manipulating and self-centered, you would not have believed us. So we said nothing." Studying his face, Georgia continued, "Now tell me about this woman and her little girl. You do realize when you fall for a woman with a child, there's always going to be an entanglement with the child's father?"

"I only met Ellen this trip." His eyes held hers. "I believe Ellen is much like you, strong, calm, and elegant." A faraway look came into his eyes. "She wears these pearls, and she speaks in the most mesmerizing voice, a mix of soft and … I can't explain it, but I can hear it in my head." He gave a self-conscious laugh. "Sounds nuts, me saying that, doesn't it?"

"No, I told you I can still hear Bill giving me advice, making me press on." She studied him for a moment. "You seem serious about this girl. Are you thinking she is the one you want to build a life with?" Her eyes shone with the concern she felt for him. "You have forgotten Madonna?"

He grinned. "Yeah, but convincing her is the thing. Madonna is completely out of my head. Thank God. This one, however, never leaves my thoughts. Like I said, I can hear her voice, and I can't forget those eyes. Did I tell you she is smart and beautiful …"

Georgia rose from the chair. "Since we are both hearing voices, maybe we should close that subject and get on to the board meeting. Some of the staff want to review what the press said about Hutson's grand opening." She stopped to lay a hand on his. "I wish you well, Daniel, and I will pray God gives you the wisdom to know whether to pursue this woman."

"I think it is too late for wisdom, though there's not a doubt in that direction. It's myself." He gave his aunt that infectious grin. "I seem to have fallen, hook, line, and sinker. I want you to meet her, and then you will understand why."

The opening was a success, according to the press release. There was no cause for concern. The staff of Hutson Hall convened early, and Georgia had errands to run.

One arm dangled over the steering wheel, Daniel waited outside in the Deville. He offered to go inside the cleaners, but his aunt insisted she needed to ask Mr. Belton about a stain on the front of the dress she wore to the opening.

"Lily," she rolled her eyes in the telling. "Madonna's mother, of all people, bumped my arm. I declare I believe it was intentional." She had sighed, shaking her head, "Those Millions never change. Did I ever tell you, Lily set her cap for Bill, and then went on to Bart Million, believing he had more money. Bart's family lost a fortune in their boating business, but somehow Bart was able to bounce back in textiles." Daniel shuddered at stories about Madonna he was just now hearing.

A young lady walked by, reminding him of Ellen. He wondered if he dared call. Shumacher might answer, or that moonstruck girl named Jenny. Somehow all the blonde jokes applied to her. But Ellen was a breath of fresh air. The man in the Deville mirror seemed to be smiling foolishly at him. Why was it when he thought of her he had such a lighthearted feeling, a smile in his heart?

No matter where he was or what he was doing, she appeared in his thoughts. There were few avenues his mind had not crossed when it came to Ellen. She was neither spit nor polish, as the old saying goes. She almost bordered on shy and old-fashioned. The clothes she wore fit in any age. The pearls drew him to her. His mother wore pearls. He remembered sitting in the crook of her arm, one hand holding the pearls where they rested in the hollow of her throat. Elizabeth Marie Hutson, wife of Dane Thorton Gates, he mused, gone too soon from her young son's life, to be buried beside her husband in a small town cemetery less than ten miles from where he was sitting.

It was foolhardy, Bill told him on more than one occasion. "Dane thought he could beat the train, pulled right into its path. They both died needlessly. Good thing you weren't with them, son." Three stones, three people Daniel loved lay in the family plot: Elizabeth, Dane, and Bill. Three years had passed since Bill died and five since Madonna had ended their engagement to marry his high school buddy. Now she tells him she is divorced. Madonna compared to Ellen made no sense. She was ruthless. Ellen in the short time he had known her seemed to be a gentle but focused individual. He wasn't sure what he had seen opening night that so intrigued and amused him when she saw the glitter and glamour of Hutson's. Madonna's jaded interest had always expected more. "Difference of oil and water," Bill used to say about many things.

She said she had a little girl, and when he pressed to meet the child, she only smiled. Would the child look like her mother? He could see Ellen, peering back at him from behind a stack of shoes at Shumachers. She seemed to always be on her knees. Taking time to study her, he had memorized her features clothed in gray with ivory satin blouses and pearls. A wisp of hair often escaped the updo, allowing her to appear gentle with a touch of vulnerability ... but, he bet, step into matters of the heart, and she would be as protective of her cub as any mother. He had to chuckle.

He hoped there was a longing in her world of responsibility that was interested, even curious to know him. What was her story, anyway? He breathed deep, seeing eyes that mocked him from the mirror. "What's your problem, buddy?" he whispered. In his heart he realized, time was short. He had to return to his business, although there were plans in the making to transfer to another city, or at least set up shop, maybe here. Could he persuade Ellen in this short amount of time that they had a future together?

Turning as Georgia emerged from the cleaners carrying three white-enveloped garments, Daniel exited the Deville to offer assistance. In the back entrance that ran between the cleaners and Hope's Beautifying Salon, he saw a man scrubbing grime from a black Suburban. The man seemed none too happy and easily noticeable as he kicked first one tire, then stepping to the next kicked it also.

Grinning, Daniel got back in the Deville, pointing toward the man, as he said, "I think we are all getting weary of this snow, don't you, Aunt Harriet?"

A chuckle rumbled in her chest. "He appears to be quite tired of it."

―――

SCRUBBING VIGOROUSLY, GARCIA WIPED SMUDGES off the mirror of the SUV. Black was beautiful when it was clean, and nothing when it was grungy. Snow had been pushed alongside the curbs. It was the slosh of the cinders in the ruts last week that had spewed slush layer by layer on the Sub.

The old van wouldn't crank this weather. The old hag had a mind of her own, like Onie.

"Where you going, hon?" she'd asked.

He couldn't say, "Surveillance, babe."

Onie always had an opinion. The boss said, don't even tell your mother when the pickup is going down. Garcia didn't have a mother. Like Onie, his mother had given him away when he was seven, but he'd run away and been on his own ever since.

Yeah, a kid could survive on his own, if he knew the right people. Take Belton's Cleaners. Who knew it was a front for illicit trade? Yes sir, many a deal went down there, unbeknownst to Belton or the cops. Belton's son knew the ropes. He got the customers, made the deals, and tied up loose ends. What daddy didn't know didn't hurt him. The son's business had nothing to do with dry cleaning. Word had it, he had made a few international deals. Now that was dangerous. Right here, in small town America, was a front for selling to kids overseas. Who would believe it? Garcia wanted no part of that.

"Don't know why I'm even doing this," Garcia muttered. "Who cares?" He threw the rags in the trash can. "Gonna have to check on the old dames, then the mommy, and figure out when's a good time to grab the kid."

CHAPTER 9

Ruthie was asleep upstairs. On the porch, Bitty and Harriet hurried against the cold, hanging lights along the porch edge, trying to finish before Ruthie awakened. Harriet held the ladder while Bitty climbed up to place the lights onto small hooks pushed under the roof's edge.

"Land's sake, our breath has turned to vapor," Bitty exclaimed, huffing a bit as she climbed down the last time. "Now, I better get this ladder back in the basement."

Once they were settled to the kitchen table, each with a mug of hot chocolate in their hands, Harriet said, "Ordinarily I wouldn't ask, but I've been wondering, doesn't Ruthie have grandparents, on either side?" She paused, contemplating her next words, "Mind you, I'm not criticizing Ellen, but …"

"I love that girl like she was mine," Bitty replied, giving a deep sigh. "I met Ellen's parents, nice people, but they saw through Jeffrey Anderson right off the reel, I'd say. Kept their mouths shut till the strain on Ellen became so evident. I suppose any good parent would step in, but Ellen wasn't buying it, and Jeffrey had filled her head full, saying they didn't like him and a million other things. Ellen loved her man."

"So there was a split," Harriet nodded. "I thought so; how long ago was this?"

"Ruthie wasn't born." Bitty replied. "When it all came down to the divorce, I practically pleaded with Ellen to call her parents."

"'Bitty,' she said. 'It's all water under the bridge. If I called them now, they'd think it was because I needed financial help. I can't do it, and Bitty, you don't either.'"

"Were you tempted?"

"There were times, I saw Ellie suffering over Jeffrey, I wanted to, but I didn't."

"And they haven't checked on her since?" Harriet's asked at length.

"Yes, but Ellen just let the letters go back, and she didn't answer the phone."

"I don't know what to make of this." Harriet gave Bitty a worried glance. "Our golden girl." It kind of stuck in Harriet's throat. "So loving and giving, believing in her Lord; but she has problems too, although this one is different than the others."

"We know the true meaning of Christmas, and yet our hearts are heavy," Salena mumbled under her breath. "I don't know how much longer I can bear this."

"It's going to be all right, Sal," James replied. He continued hanging red and green ornaments on the higher branches. Ways to comfort his wife were running scarce. Born Salena Elizabeth Dock, his wife of thirty years had been nicknamed Sal by an old traveling salesman in the days of her youth as he called on her parents' farm. The story was told to him by Salena's mother.

"The old man would come for orders. When our daughter was born, he came in to see her and he asked her name. Salena Elizabeth Dock, I said. That's too long, she'll never learn how to spell it, he said. I'll just call her Sally, and every time he came he saw Salena and called her Sally. Then when the neighbor's boys were born and they learned to talk, they shortened her name to Sal."

Funny how life happens, James thought as he stepped back to view his work. "Perfect," he said. "Top branches are finished. You ready to eat lunch? I've been tasting that roast ever since I came here to help you decorate the tree. The aroma has made me hungry."

"How do you know it's roast?"

He grinned, "Because when I walked through the kitchen I lifted the lid." Big as he was, James whirled around to lift Sally off the floor and up into his arms. That's when he saw the tears in her eyes.

"Oh, Sal, let it go. It's eating you up. You have got to turn loose of it."

"I can't, James." Sal tucked her head against his chest, feeling his arms tighten around her body. Here, in James' arms, she felt sheltered and comforted. For a moment she allowed that need to be fed. Finally she said, "You can put me down. I'll set dinner on the table."

He nuzzled his chin against the top of her head. "Maybe I don't want to put you down." James sank into the nearest chair with Sal on his lap. "Honey, you've started losing weight again. I can tell. You are light as a feather."

"It's almost Christmas. I think of Ellie more through the holidays, wondering where she is, what she is doing, and sometimes even who she is with." Sally tightened her arms around her husband's neck. "Now I know we should never have interfered."

"All we did was warn her," James insisted. "I don't call that interfering when it's your very own daughter." He shook his head, stubborn. "Worst thing for him was when we went a day early and caught him in bed with another woman." Shifting, uncomfortable with the memory, he swallowed, trying to push the anger down to a slow simmer he could never forget. "I wanted to beat the daylights out of him." Now James grinned, "Then when I told Ellie and she didn't believe me, I wanted to whip her."

"Shh." Sally peered into his eyes. "You never laid a hand on Ellie all your life. She had you wrapped around her little finger. I had to do the disciplining."

"Not much discipline. She was a good girl." James sighed. "Why are we doing this, Sal? What's it been, almost four years since we've seen Ellen, and you still insist we put a tree up every year, just in case she comes home? Then you weep through Christmas." James drew a deep breath; it hurt him too. "Remember what Pastor Cook said; you raise up a child in the ways they should go, and they will return to you?"

"I try to hang on to that," Sal said. "It's like I can't give up hope."

James stared into the depth of Sal's eyes. "Yeah, I know, but does Ellen?" It appeared to him, in comforting each other, they had changed roles. "We can look for her again, Sal, but it's up to Ellen whether she wants us in her life. So what good would it do?"

Later, as Sally dried the dinner dishes and straightened the kitchen, she wondered if Ellen was happy. How could she be? She was without parents that loved her. Ellen met Jeffrey in her first year of college. Aware of Jeffrey's reputation, they asked her to go slow. But as they watched, Jeffrey swept their daughter off her feet, married her the next year, and moved Ellen across town. Quickly she and James learned, Jeffrey wanted her all to himself, and Ellen was flattered, completely unaware of Jeff's words to her parents: "I don't mean to sound rude, but my business is taking off, and since Ellie takes care of the books, we do have a schedule. I hope when you want to visit you will be mindful of that."

"I doubt she ever knew," Sal mumbled under her breath. It was when James had been to the lumber shed for supplies to repair their porch, he overheard talk about Jeff. Storming through the screen door, leaving it to bang shut, flushed and agitated, James paced the floor. "He's having an affair with Cal Steven's daughter," James announced, "the banker's girl, for heaven's sake. What does he think, the whole world won't know? Ellie won't find out?"

Confronted, Jeffrey neither denied nor fabricated lies concerning his affair. "I've been offered a housing project to build in Martindale," he said. "Ellen and I are moving."

James said he had gritted his teeth and thrown his hat on Jeff's desk. "Good Lord, man, are you completely insane? This is my daughter. You don't even acknowledge wrongdoing, and then you tell me you are moving. Do you care anything about Ellen?"

Jeff had shrugged. "Do you? We could use some help moving."

Out of sight, out of mind simply was not true. Sally thought of her daughter daily, sometimes on the hour, and hard as she tried not to, she relived James' telling of the incident, which only brought more pain. It was Ellen's unscheduled trip to the dentist that day that caused her to discover Jeffrey's latest indiscretion, but Ellen took her marriage vows seriously.

Only after a matter of time, Ellie realized Jeffrey never intend to stop. By then, she had severed contact with her parents. While the sadness of the situation tore at their being, together, Sally and James learned peace comes only through one's walk with God. Ellie was the trophy of their lives; her absence left a great void. They questioned, tormented themselves, asked why this had happened, and in general made themselves sick in heart and soul.

It was James who finally said, "Once before, it was when we gave up and put our lives in God's hands, something grand and glorious happened."

Sally considered James. When he said she was losing weight, it was true. She supposed her grieving over Christmas, and another year of unanswered prayer, to be the reason she had no appetite. In the early years of their marriage when they wanted to start a family, nothing happened. Suffering through the months that evolved into years, James had drawn her close to his side and asked, "Sally, why don't we turn this completely over to God?" Putting a finger to her protesting lips, James continued, "I know, we say we have, but that's just lip service. So, let's be happy we have each other and spend our days thanking God for what we do have. Then if he sees fit to grant a little baby into our lives, we will be ready."

Bowing her head, Sally felt ashamed. True, she gave the problem to God, but she kept taking it back, hoping to solve it, not waiting for God's timing. James was right, but oh, it was not easy. Still, it was a sin to let anything destroy you to the point of hurting your body, even with a simple little thing like weight loss, wasn't it? She would never have thought she was that foolish. But worry packs a heavy wallop. *And trial brings strength …* wasn't that what her mother always said? "I'm so tired of strength training," she muttered.

"It's almost Christ Church day," Ruthie whispered as she wrapped her doll in a dishtowel. "Now when we go, we have to be very, very quiet. I whispered last week." Cradling the doll in the crook of her arm, she rocked back and forth on the sofa. "You must not cry, Elis-za-beth, just listen to the man talk about Jesus."

"Elizabeth, huh?" Bitty wiped a cloth around the base of the lamp. "Where did you find that name?"

"I don't know. Is it mommy's sister?"

"Mommy doesn't have a sister."

"Does she have a mommy?"

"I have to check a burner on the stove," Bitty said, moving toward the kitchen.

Ruthie followed. "Does mommy have a mommy?"

"I don't know."

"If she doesn't have a sister, maybe she doesn't have a mommy or daddy, like me."

"But you have a daddy." Bitty lingered in the doorway.

"No. He forgot me." Ruthie patted the doll and kissed Elizabeth on the head. "It's okay. Mommy can get me another daddy someday."

"Now what would you know about that?"

Ruthie lay Elizabeth down on the couch. "I don't. But if my daddy don't want me, maybe someone else will. If he likes mommy, then he can like me too."

Shaking her head, Bitty returned to the stove. The beans were boiling away. She had a ham hock to add and later this evening planned to bake the old iron skillet full of corn bread.

"Do you think Miss Harriet will come eat with us? I miss her."

Bitty chuckled. Whoever would have thought it, she missed Harriet too.

"We are going to Christ Church, aren't we, Bitty?" Ruthie's face lit up with such an inner glow of happiness that she slapped her hands together. "Art you just so happy, Bitty? We can see the baby Jesus in waddled clothes laying in the manger, but Mommy said I can't hold him."

"*Aren't*," Bitty corrected. "And it is *swaddling* clothes. Baby Jesus was wrapped in swaddling clothes. They didn't have gowns ... or diapers ... I guess, so they wrapped cloths around the baby." For a moment, Bitty set her mouth in a firm line that told Ruthie she was thinking. "Ruthie, would you be upset if I don't go to Christ Church this Sunday?"

"Why?" Ruthie's happy face dissolved into sadness, a pout rounding out her lips. "Can't we all sit together and sing and look at baby Jesus again?"

"I'm thinkin' on it, baby girl, but I just don't think I will go this time."

"You got to go, Bitty." Ruthie reached up to clasp Bitty's neck, pulling her down. "You got to go to Christ Church. It's impertent."

"*Important*," Bitty corrected.

"That too." Momentarily the sadness lifted as Ruthie grinned. "Can I have another dishcloth, Bitty. My baby needs to wear waddling clothes."

"*Swaddling*." Opening the drawer, taking out another cloth, Bitty shook her head wearily. "Swaddling."

CLOSING THE CASH REGISTER, ELLEN glanced through the shop window and down the hall to a glimmer of daylight at the front entrance to the mall. Everyone was ready for the snow to lift, but warnings of rain, dropping temperatures, and additional snow to follow had not lightened the atmosphere. Rain would wash away the grime of ash the road department used that was literally coating the vehicles and darkening the mall floors, but rain? She sighed. It was dark and dreary, and the days of extra hours were catching up with her. Absent minded, she studied her hands where defective tabs had left traces of ink. At the time she could not go to the back room to clean them, but now with no one in the shop she would.

"Hello, beautiful." Daniel stood there as she returned from the curtained area. He was holding a bouquet of roses in his hand and the most wonderful smile on his face. "For you, madame."

"Oh, they are beautiful." She felt the blush spread from her neckline into her hair, as tears brimmed in her eyes. "Thank you." Through the clear vase, the stems rested in flat marbles. "It has been years since I've received roses."

"That's a shame," he said softly. "But don't cry." Setting the roses on the counter, he handed her his handkerchief. "You should have roses more often. You shall."

"Oh no." Embarrassed, she handed the handkerchief back to Daniel. "Thank you, but there's tissue here. Thank you."

"You said that." He grinned. "I thought I should soften the next question. My aunt wants to meet you. Can you join me for dinner tomorrow night at my aunt's home?"

Feeling a sudden weakness in her knees, Ellen placed her hands on the counter. "It's Saturday night?"

"I know." He glanced around. "Won't Shumacher let you off at the usual time?" The infectious grin spread across his face. "I'll be glad to ask him."

"No. No." She protested. "I do have the night off as I traded with Jenny wanting next week to attend her friend's wedding." She hesitated. "If I can pull it all together."

"What?" He leaned forward, his hands on each side of hers on the countertop, their noses only inches apart. "I promise to have you home at a decent hour. Can you come with me after work, or better still, I will follow you home and we can go from there."

"I might ..." Before she could finish the sentence, he interrupted. His eyes narrowing, he asked, "It's not another date, is it? Say so if I am creating a problem." He swallowed, and then faltered, trying to soften his words. "If it is, just say, *get lost, buster*."

It was as if a contest of wills waged war inside of him. Amused and a bit chagrined, she had not seen this side of him. Ellen decided she liked that puzzled look on him; it told her he was very interested.

"It's hardly that," she said "I've worked so many hours this week, I haven't had time to prepare mine or Ruthie's clothes for Sunday."

"Is Sunday a date?"

"No." Now he was holding one hand up, as a teacher would silence a student. A smile wavered inside Ellen she dared not allow ... nor speak.

He seemed to be accessing the situation. First his eyes narrowed in scrutiny, holding hers until finally a mischievous gleam appeared. "Me thinks the lady is holding out on me." He rocked back on his heels, eyebrows raised. Waiting. "Preparation of clothes can't outshine meeting Aunt Georgia, can it?"

She laughed. "Actually it is church day. Ruthie is so excited, but as in everything, there is a smidgen of preparation, and I have to admit, sometimes when I return home, all I want to do is sit down, take off my shoes, and listen to Ruthie tell me about her day."

"I should acquaint you with a good shoe person," he said, "but I volunteer to rub your tired feet instead." While she rolled her eyes, he asked, "Where do you attend church?"

"Christ Church, the one with the dome." She ignored the foot part of the conversation.

"What a coincidence. My aunt is on the board of care and enrichment at Christ Church."

"Never heard of it," Ellen replied. "Are you making that up?"

"Well, I forget the correct name, but it means something about caring for people and helping those with problems, a fund of some sort. It's a biblical name, I think."

"Barnabas fund?" she offered. "It seems all denominations have that. It's named after Barnabas in the Bible who served his fellow man. It is usually maintained by offerings above one's own tithe in order to meet the needs of people with hardship."

"Aren't you just a walking encyclopedia of information?" He smirked, leaning in closer. "Now, how about I pick you up here when you get off work ... what time?" He tilted his head, waiting and grinning all the while. "Come on. Don't let me down." While she lingered, he said, "Look, I'm feeling very intimidated here. Give a man a chance."

"Seven," she said, a bit lightheaded the way he was smiling, expectant of her answer. "Now, before I get fired, scoot out of here. But, first ... tell me, what do I wear?"

"Pearls. Always the pearls." He was backing toward the door. "Churchy. Aunt Georgia is churchy dress type. And remember ... about those feet, I have an antidote."

Ellen closed the shop at nine, thankful Mr. Shumacher planned to relieve her at seven the next night. It was a weekend and he wanted no loose ends, no doors left unlocked with unchaperoned children prowling the mall, and certainly no money left in the drawer. If she had no further delays, she should arrive home in time to enjoy Bitty's good cooking.

Bitty motioned for everyone to gather around the table as she set a huge pot of beans in the center of the table, followed by an iron skillet of corn bread. "Harriet, if you will pour the tea, I will bring the slaw, and Ellen, you might want those pickles out of the fridge."

"How are you holding up?" Harriet asked. "Lot of hours working, I hear."

"Two until seven on concrete, nine tonight; that floor is a killer. My feet feel like watermelons."

"You should work for someone that sells good shoes," Harriet joked. "Tell old Shu, Harriet Becker said it's time to put in a line that is both comfortable and pretty."

"You know my boss?"

"Anne said not to wait," Bitty interrupted. "She will eat when she gets here. So I guess we are ready as soon as you bless the food, Ellen."

"Father in heaven, we are thankful and ask your blessing on the food and Bitty who has prepared it for us. We ask for your guidance and your watch care over our lives as we go about each day. It is in your holy name, we ask. Amen."

"What's watch care?"

"It means," Ellen explained, "wherever we are, whatever we are doing, God is there." Ruthie seemed to accept her answer. Ellen turned to Harriet, "You know Mr. Shumacher?"

Nodding, Harriet dipped beans and ham into Ellen and Ruthie's plates, waiting as Bitty cut the cornbread and distributed it. "Honey, you would be surprised the people I know in this town. Mr. Becker was very affluent. We partied with the best." She sighed. "It was after he died, I backed away from everyone. Most were pretty good Joes, like Shu, but now and then I encountered a real pain in the you know what."

She grinned, turning to Bitty, "I declare, you can take three dishes and outshine any restaurant up town."

Tugging on Ellen's sleeve, Ruthie asked, "What's you know what?"

While Bitty and Harriet hid behind their napkins, Ellen explained, "It is sometimes used when we don't know the name of something. Now how was your day, Sweetums?"

"Let me show you." Ruthie slid off her chair. "You need to know this." She turned toward the door as Anne arrived. "You need to know this too, Anne." Ruthie lay down on the floor, scooting on her stomach toward the living room door. "It was on Dora. If your house catches on fire, don't hide in the closet, don't get under the bed. Look for the nearest door and scoot to it. If you can't get it open, look for a window, and if you can't get it open, break it."

"What do I do after I open the window?"

"Holler." Ruthie climbed back onto her chair, put her hands to her mouth, and hollered, "Bitty, come get me."

Hugging Ruthie to her body, Ellen shook with laughter. "Ruth Elizabeth Anderson, I never know what to expect from you."

"We did it, didn't we, Bitty?" Ruthie beamed. "Me and Bitty. Today we learned what to do if the house is on fire. Dora told us." She clapped her hands. "You want to do it again, Bitty, me and you in the floor?"

All eyes turned to Bitty. Bitty rolled her eyes. "A little training doesn't hurt anyone." Taking up a fork, she said, "Now, let's eat."

"Tomorrow night, Ruthie," Anne said, "'Rudolph the Red Nosed Reindeer' is on."

"Umm." Ruthie's mouth was full, and she was trying to spread butter on corn bread.

"Let me help, Sweetums." Ruthie watched Ellen spread the butter.

"It's easier when you do it. Can you watch Rudolph too, Mommy?"

"I work until seven."

"It begins at six," Anne said. "How about I bring Andy, since I get him this weekend for his visit, and we can watch it? You, Bitty, Andy, and me?"

Ruthie clapped her hands. "Then, next day we go to Christ Church. Right, Bitty?"

She waited for Bitty's answer, but it did not come. "We made a colander, didn't we?" Ruthie's face wore a puzzled expression. "Didn't we?"

"Yes, a *calendar*." Bitty agreed, nodding.

"We all go to Christ Church on Sunday, don't we, Bitty?"

Later, as Bitty ran hot water in the sink, Harriet placed dirty dishes on the side.

"Don't look so worried."

"What do you mean? I am not worried."

"Don't pull that innocent act with me. I saw the expression on your face when Ruthie said we were all going to church." Picking up a fresh dishtowel, Harriet stared at Bitty. "Is there any particular reason you do not wish to go to church this Sunday?"

"Well, I feel ashamed to admit it, and I wasn't going to discuss it. You know there is nothing I wouldn't do for Ellen and Ruthie, but I'm just not ready for this church …"

"Attendance?" Harriet nodded. "I'm a little hesitant too. But something is drawing me back." A sad expression crossed her face. "There are things in my life …" She sighed. "I can't go into that either. Mr. Becker always said, 'Forget your past, and embrace the future. What happened to you when you were young is no one's business.'"

Bitty's hands stilled as she turned to Harriet. "Do you want to talk …?"

"No. I can't go into it. Maybe someday I can, but not now."

CHAPTER 10

It was zero degrees, Garcia was thinking, shifting uncomfortably beneath the window, his listening post, where he was hidden by an old swing with a frozen afghan thrown over the back. Someone had thought to remove the swing from the ceiling hooks and set it on the floor through the winter months. There he lay, hearing the old women yak. The cold had already claimed his bones, and his feet felt like lead, but this was possibly his last stakeout. He'd been warned if he didn't finish the job this weekend, someone else would, and with what he knew, they would have to figure out what to do about him.

Then there was Onie, threatening to set him out on the street. She was near nuts needing a fix. If he wasn't involved in kidnapping the little girl, he'd leave. Like they said, he knew too much. Onie was ready to pounce. She'd been in rehab, and that had accomplished nothing. "I got a past full of regrets," she explained. "If you had to live with what's in my head, you'd try to forget too."

As if she knew his past. He'd had to learn to make do with what people laid on him. Spoiled food, from trash cans, until he was old enough to be the street courier. Yeah, a fancy name for delivery boy, he remembered. Delivering for the big guys who lived in fancy houses, went about their daily business, hiding in the shadows of night when they did their dirty work. Sometimes he wondered were there any legitimate people. Somehow all he knew were crooks. He remembered the day he asked the fat cat in the three-piece suit what was his job. He'd just been hired.

"Courier," the fat cat answered. "Get the goods, get out of there. Bring it to me." If he ever had a chance, Garcia French might turn his life around. Fat chance.

The worst thing here was whoever was behind this job said there was another waiting to do what he'd failed, as yet, to do. Nervous, he removed a glove and chewed on a fingernail. Was that a lie, or was there another person? All he had met was the boss. If he wasn't mistaken, the boss was wearing a fake hairpiece, and he'd bet a dollar the man didn't wear glasses. Everything was a cover-up … the man's protection so he was never recognized. Then who was the emphysema guy? Nothing was fair in life. They knew him. He didn't know them. Guess who would get caught with kidnapping charges if anything went wrong. Bingo.

Just this morning, Onie called. "Get outta bed, Garcia French." She turned the volume on the television louder. "That little girl in Oklahoma ain't been found, and they're talking about kidnapping charges against the kid's next door neighbor, and he ain't nothing but an accomplice."

"What can they prove?" Garcia asked. "What's their evidence?"

"I don't know, hon. But you better be careful."

—→ ←—

ANNE WAS STUDYING. UPSTAIRS, ELLEN shut the door to her room, readying Ruthie for bed. "Come on, Sweetums, let me brush your hair, and after that roll in the floor, I guess you need another bath."

"Don't," Ruthie grumbled. "Bitty mopped today and I'm still clean."

"We might negotiate to a wipe down with the wash cloth and clean pajamas."

"What's nugtiate?" Ruthie sat in front of her mother, listening to the sound of the brush whispering through her hair.

"*Negotiate* means you and I come to an agreement. I want something, you want something different, so we think of a way to solve our problem."

"I needed that word when I was telling Bitty something today."

Ellen grinned. "Is it a secret, or can you tell me?"

Yawning, Ruthie slid away from her mother. "You won't like it and I'm tired."

"Well, little cross bear, just give me a minute to get that wash cloth and you can go to sleep."

By the time Ellen returned, Ruthie was sound asleep and did not waken while her mother wiped her feet clean and put on fresh pajamas. Smiling, Ellen could only wonder what Ruthie thought she would not like. A secret in the making, she guessed.

The next morning rain was drumming on the roof. For a moment, Ellen lay listening. The monthlong weather was wearing on everyone's nerves. Driving in it was not for the novice. She had to climb out of bed. The drive was one thing, but she must take time to search her wardrobe for something fitting to wear to meet Daniel's aunt. Her social life had been in such a lull, she could not think of anything proper for the occasion. If she were expected to wear a garment near the splendor of Hutson's opening, she should stay home.

With a pain of guilt, she remembered she had not had opportunity to tell Ruthie. She had gone back down stairs to tell Bitty and to see if there were any problems for Bitty staying, and felt she had walked in on private conversation between Bitty and

Harriet. Harriet was saying she had things in her life, but had not finished the sentence when Ellen walked in. They were all struggling with something, it seemed, but an unspoken agreement allowed each to work out their problem without interference.

Now as she dressed for work, Ellen wondered whether meeting Daniel's aunt a good thing. When he kissed her, she had felt underlying emotions. The memory lingered; not even Jeffrey had been that gentle nor had stirred her body to react. She supposed he had at one time, but Jeffrey had done a good job of destroying their love. She shook her head, touching her lips as if the feeling were still there. It was, after all, a short kiss.

Bitty was pouring a cup of coffee for herself when Ellen entered the kitchen. A pan of fresh muffins sat on the stove top. "Oh, Bitty, didn't I tell you to sleep in? I don't have to go in until nine, but with the rain I thought I should leave soon. Mr. Shumacher said he would open; an old friend was dropping by and he wanted to be there."

"You told me, but I promised Ruthie I would have blueberry muffins this morning."

"She is still asleep." Ellen grinned. "It must be the rain on the rooftop."

"Weather man says it will turn to sleet and snow this evening." Bitty set the pan of muffins on the table and asked, "You want coffee or milk?"

"Beatrice, sit down. Let me serve you for once. You are not the hired hand. You are my friend." Ellen gave Bitty a hug while planting a kiss on her cheek. "You spoil us."

Grinning, Bitty said, "Well, I'm just happy you notice. It's been such rough weather, I don't think I would have liked being clear across town by myself."

"What would we do without you?" Ellen spoke around a mouthful of muffin. "Ummm. No one can hold a candle to you. You should enter a contest."

They turned as Ruthie came, bare feet, padding into the room. "I smelled something good all the way up there." She leaned into Ellen's side for a hug, then went to Bitty. "Is it blueberry, Bitty?"

"You bet your muffin." Bitty gave her a kiss on the head. "Just sit right there."

"You didn't go to work," Ruthie said, liking her mother at the table.

"No, I have something to tell you and see if you approve."

"Is it a secret?"

"No." Ellen reached across to straighten Ruthie's hair. "You know tonight is Saturday night."

"And tomorrow is Christ Church day." Happy, Ruthie turned to Bitty. "Can I have another muffin? This one's almost gone." She giggled. "Almost."

"May I have another muffin," Ellen corrected.

"Yes, can't she, Bitty?" Ruthie smiled into Ellen's face. "What's your secret?" she whispered.

Laughing, Ellen said, "No secret. Do you mind if I accept an invitation to dinner to meet someone?"

"Remember, Bitty, what I told you." Ruthie clapped her hands. "I told you."

Behind Ruthie's back, the two women grinned and rolled their eyes. "How old are you?" Ellen asked.

"I'm three, but I feel like four."

"I thought so," Ellen teased. "So what do you think? Is it all right if I go? And when I come home tonight, we need to see if you can still wear that tea-length dress from last year that was too big. If it fits, you can wear it Sunday."

Ruthie clapped her hands. "To Christ Church." Leaning toward Bitty, she clasped an arm around Bitty's neck and whispered in her ear.

"She wants to know the name of the person you are meeting."

Puzzled, Ellen replied. "Georgia, but I don't know the last name."

Disappointed, Ruthie's shoulders drooped. "I thought Georgia was a country."

"Where is this conversation headed?" Rising, Ellen paused by the chair. "Sweetums, Georgia is a state, but it can be a person's name." She shook her head. "I declare, Beatrice, you sure have a job cut out for you, but you must be doing something right if she thought Georgia was a country. She is just three years old."

Ellen left with a garment bag looped over her shoulder and a small cosmetic case in her hand. She did not feel at ease leaving work later that evening without the means to freshen her body and change out of the gray suit she was wearing, nor to wear the items in the bag to work.

"It's a strange world, Beatrice," she muttered as Bitty stood ready to close the door behind her. "We should write a book, but *Desperate Women* already exists."

Arriving at five, Jenny whispered, "There was an accident down on Fifth and Main. I thought I was going to have to call in, but the cops cleared my lane."

"Anyone we know?"

"Haven't heard names, but it was bad."

Shumacher appeared near seven. "Are you still leaving, Ellen?" She swallowed, nervously. "Yes, sir, if you don't need me."

Shumacher turned to the door. "I'll be down the hall until then."

"You talkin' to me?" Jennie whispered in her Segal voice. "He doesn't even know my name. Jenny. Jenny. Jenny." Hands on hips, she mouthed to his back.

The clocks started chiming in Rutherford clock shop down the hall. Ellen scurried away. "I need a few minutes in the back," she called over her shoulder.

"Hey, got a hot date?" Jenny giggled. "I hope he's not hiding back there."

A mist of this, a spray of that, touch up of the makeup, and a quick brush through the hair, Ellen was pulling the long, black skirt over the rose chiffon blouse when she heard Jenny purring. "You girl. Purrr." She giggled softly. "Come out. Come out, wherever you are ... or, all's fair in love and war."

No one could miss Jenny circling Daniel as he stood waiting, with a hint of amusement in his eyes. Ellen came from the curtained area carrying a short velvet cut jacket in her hands. Now Daniel's eyes were glued on Ellen in a most admiring way, and no one could miss the glow of happiness that lit his face. "Hi, beautiful," he said, not caring Jenny was soaking it up, and the room had suddenly filled with customers.

"Let me help you with the jacket."

Jenny's mouth fell open as he waited for Ellen to slip her arms in, then he pulled her hair free, lifted it to touch and center the pearls she wore, and turned Ellen to face him. "Perfect," he said. Just as Ellen would kiss the top of Ruthie's hair, in tenderness, he kissed Ellen's hair.

"Lord, have mercy. I think I'm going to faint." Jenny fanned ceremoniously. "Are there any more of you out there? Do you have a brother, a cousin, even?"

"'Fraid not," Daniel laughed, good naturedly. "Nice to see you." He gave a gentleman's nod, took Ellen's hand, and said, "Have I told you that you look marvelous?" Ellen would remember later, for some reason, the customers cheered.

———

"Aunt Georgia, meet Ellen Anderson." Daniel rocked back on his heels, evidently proud of both women.

"My dear, you are lovely," his aunt said, "and refreshing, I might add."

"How's that, Aunt Georgia?"

Georgia Hutson was leading the way to the dining room, the table set with platinum-ringed white china, silver gleaming by each setting, and a bouquet of pink roses sprinkled with baby's breath in a low vase centered on the table.

"Well, let me explain. Somehow, I knew," she smiled, "when you told me Ellen reminded you of me, I just knew she would not come wearing a dress twelve inches above the knee." She smiled. "You sit there, Ellen, so we can hear each other, Daniel on my right, you on my left."

Daniel first helped his aunt and then Ellen be seated as she continued, "Now, isn't this cozy?" She picked up a napkin, placing it in her lap. "You look very pretty, Ellen."

"Thank you." Ellen was at a loss for words. Here she sat in her outdated or as some might say, timeless, wardrobe, while she had walked through a beautifully decorated home, with oils on the walls, sparkling chandeliers, and foot-deep carpets. She took a few deep breaths to hold at bay the feeling of intimidation, praying she would not embarrass herself as a guest, or her hostess, in the present nervous state of her mind.

"Now tell me about yourself. Daniel says you have a young daughter." With that she rang a small crystal bell. "I don't usually have Rosie serve, but she insisted. I turned my ankle the day before Hutson's opening. Well, that kept me down a few days, then thinking it well, evidently I was up on it too soon, and now it's swollen again. So," she smiled as Rosie came through the door, "my friend came over. She cooked and I sat and talked."

"Ellen, this is my friend of twenty-seven years. Rosie and I have raised husbands and her babies together, and we have both buried the loves of our lives." Rosie smiled, making a nod and excused herself to the kitchen.

"What do you mean you raised your husbands?" Daniel asked.

"Well, you don't think a man evolves all by himself, do you?" She patted his hand. "But it's all right. It's an act of love." She sighed. "When they are gone, you miss them something terrible." She became busy, forking through her salad.

"Of course, I'm joking, Daniel," she grinned. "Now, Ellen, what about you?"

"There's not a lot to tell. Presently I am working toward being a RN. I do have a three-year-old daughter, and I'm blessed with a wonderful woman who cares for Ruthie."

"Daniel said he met you at Shumachers."

"Let me tell this," Daniel said, teasing laughter in his eyes. "Little did I know Shumacher had this lovely lady working there. I left my boots at home and when I arrived to ten inches of snow on the ground, I knew that had to be corrected. I found this divine creature down on her knees stacking shoe boxes, and I've been smitten ever since." He grinned, unabashed. "It must be a mystical spell, because I find myself thinking about her all the time, shaving, walking down the stairs, even driving on the street."

"That could be dangerous." Georgia Hutson solemnly studied the two, first Daniel on her right, and then Ellen on her left. "I'm afraid, in all these years, I've never heard this poetic rendition from my nephew." Pursing her mouth just so, she asked, "How do you feel about that, Ellen?"

Rosie's appearance, carrying a large steaming casserole, saved Ellen answering. While across the table, Daniel continued to smile, knowing her distress, he said, "Saved by the bell, huh?"

Georgia reached over to pat the top of Ellen's hand. "We know, they love to embarrass us, don't we? Think nothing of it. You can get even later."

Rosie gave Daniel a double portion. "Oh, boy, Rosie, you remembered," he said. "It smells wonderful."

"I thought about steak, but Georgia remembered, this was always Daniel's favorite." To Ellen she explained, "It is chicken breast baked in rice with green pepper, mushroom, and celery soup poured over," she grinned, "plus a few other secret ingredients." She placed a hand on Daniel's shoulder. "I've known this boy about as long as Georgia."

"Can you sit with us too?" Georgia asked. "You've worked all evening."

"Let me bring in the vegetable dish, and I'll set the dessert on the sideboard, then I will join you." The remaining part of the meal was spent in light banter as they shared fun times, and laughter erupted around the table. Ellen found herself enjoying the two and found the beginning nervousness was completely unnecessary.

"Once," Georgia said, "due to a traffic problem where the funeral procession we were in was divided, and our line held long enough to lose the car in front of us, we finally pulled into this cemetery and there appeared to be two burials in progress. But there is a car just down the lane, and Rosie says she will just jump out and ask the driver if this is where so-and-so is being buried. It turned out … she comes running back, sputtering, "Go. Go. Just drive.""

The two laughed, remembering. "It so happened, the people in the car were not there for a burial at all. Oh my word, it was not even the man's wife, and we knew both of them. For some reason we were laughing so hard by then, we could not go to the cemetery anyway." Georgia dabbed at her eyes where laughter had brought tearing. "Anyway, that was our funniest experience. Don't ask me why."

"And," Rosie added, "whenever we saw any of the four thereafter, we always wondered if either of the two couples had any idea about their spouse's indiscretion." She sighed. "Georgia, maybe that isn't a story we should tell a dating couple."

It was nearly nine when they drove out of the drive, and Ellen glanced back to see his aunt standing at the window waving to them. "She loves you very much."

"I know," he said. "She and Uncle Bill became my second parents."

The Deville slid, momentarily, as he corrected. "This is just what the weather man predicted, rain turning to snow and sleet, leaving a thin layer of ice beneath it." He pressed the radio button. Listening, Ellen heard the announcer say, "An accident at Fifth and Main took the life of a young woman this afternoon. The victim has been identified as Merelee Fith, a nursing student, who was killed when a second car slammed into the driver side of her vehicle. Meanwhile, city workers strive to—"

Ellen gasped, struggling to breathe. "I know her. She is in most of my classes." She felt as though someone socked her in the throat, cutting off all her air. "I can't believe she is gone." She struggled not to cry as Daniel reached for her hand, to hold for a moment before returning his hand back to the steering wheel.

"I am sorry. The condition of this road is treacherous." A ragged sigh escaped as he saw her shoulders heaving. "There is always the shock," his voice was gentle. "Death does pack a wallop. I wish I knew words to comfort you."

"We were not close friends, but sharing classes, we have been through a lot together. Merelee kept us all from going crazy." Her voice trembled into a sob. "She could say what we were all thinking and get by with it. She had this fun way about her. You could tell the instructors liked her." Pressing her hands to her face, Ellen's words came muffled. "I'm sorry. I just feel like crying."

"If these roads weren't so terrible, I'd like to hold your hand ... or you, and just let you cry" he replied. "Why don't you let me drive you home? We could pick up your car tomorrow."

"That's probably wise," she agreed. "We will go to church in Anne's car anyway." Ellen sank into miserable silence.

Subdued himself, Daniel did not disturb her. No doubt she was thinking the same thing could happen to her, and just hearing her devotion to her child, he felt she questioned if something happened to her, would her child's father pick up the pieces? He understood. When his parents died, he became an orphan, and he did not know what would have happened to him, had his aunt and uncle not stepped in to take him into their lives.

CHAPTER 11

Thankful everyone had gone to bed, Ellen sank into the leather chair by the fireplace. The curtains were open, and she watched the struggle of cars passing on the street. Merelee, gone. It was more than she could comprehend. She thought Merelee was another divorcee with a son. A ragged breath caught in her throat. Had Merielee made provision for her son? What would happen to Ruthie if anything happened to her? Wistfully, she remembered her mother saying how pleased they would be when grandchildren were added to the family.

Guilt assuaged Ellen's memory. They had been right about Jeffrey. He was unfaithful. And he could care less about the welfare of their daughter. She could imagine the belligerent expression on Jeffrey's face when he received the letter from the court saying he was responsible for child support, and if he did not pay, he would be facing a day in court, possible infringement regarding his rights, and the likelihood of incarceration if the court found him guilty. The agency had sent her a copy of the letter mailed to Jeffrey. Garnishment of wages would not sit well with Ruthie's father.

She did not know how long she sat there, until she heard the gong of the hall clock striking one. The clock had been given to Ellen when her grandmother died. "Oh, Mimmie," she whispered, "if you were only here to tell me what I must do." The small, quiet voice that had guided her since childhood whispered back, *You have your parents. It is time to put away the foolish pride and contact them. Time will not turn back, but you can go forward.* She sighed, gripping the handrail. Time was spiraling out of control.

Yawning, she donned her nightgown and climbed into bed beside Ruthie. Ruthie deserved to know her grandparents, but the undoing of a wrong could not happen overnight, and sometimes it was very painful.

SUBDUED, RUTHIE GLANCED BACK AT Bitty, an accusing expression on her face. Bitty chose not to attend Christ Church with the group, but Harriet was in high spirits. Ellen insisted Ruthie not say another word to Bitty.

"Shhh. Now hurry, get your coat on. Bitty can stay home if she wants to."

"But I want her to go."

"Doesn't matter, Sweetums," Ellen was buttoning her coat. "Here, let's straighten the bow Ms. Harriet brought you." Ruthie started to protest. "Huh-uh," Ellen cautioned. "Bitty is not going." She hugged her little daughter to her chest. "So shush."

"You look like a little doll, Ruthie," Anne said as she held onto Andy's hand, guiding him down the stairs. To Ellen she said, "I guess this is my holiday, as Andrew gets him next week. Seems the girlfriend is there and she doesn't want all the fuss made over Andy."

"I'm surprised Andrew would even tell you that. Won't she be there next weekend?"

"No, she has to go to her family in Tennessee." Anne grinned. "Yeah, Tennessee. But, I kind of suspect there's more going on."

They went out to the parking lot, Anne fastening Andy in his car seat and Ellen setting Ruthie in hers, while Harriet climbed in the front with Anne. Ellen sat between the two car seats. "Where is your car?" Anne asked. "I don't see it."

"The roads were so bad last night, I left it at the mall." Ellen nodded as Anne's eyes met hers in the visor mirror. They grinned. "So, everyone ready for church?"

Ruthie clapped, but her voice was pouty. "I still want Bitty to go with us."

"I know, Ruthie." Anne pulled out of the parking lot, "I was worried, but the city has already cleared the road. They must have worked all night."

Ellen remembered Merelee. "Remind me to tell you something later." Though she had thought about the accident earlier, she couldn't tell Anne with Ruthie listening. There would be a horde of questions from her daughter.

———◆———

BITTY ROLLED THE CHICKEN PIECES in potato flakes before placing them in the baking pan, poured celery soup over them, and set the pan on the top rack of the oven. Setting the timer for an hour and ten minutes, she walked to the window, wondering how bad the roads were. The parking lot was mostly empty. She guessed the hill's residents attended church or had left town for the weekend. Now where did one go when ice was on the ground and the roads remained dangerous in many areas? One black Suburban was parked at the back of the lot; at least it wasn't that old van with the funny little man in it Harriet had told her about. Harriet had laughed when he had hit the side of the van. "If I am not wrong, I believe he broke the handle off the driver's side door," she had said.

Sighing deeply, Bitty couldn't help thinking of Ruthie's expression upon leaving. "I just couldn't do it," she said aloud, glancing toward the ceiling. "That child looked like a little angel. That little tea-length dress finally fit, and her hair pulled up into the bow Harriet brought. Yes, ma'am. She gives Shirley Temple a run for the money. And she was so excited. You hear me, Larry." Bitty shook her fist in the air.

"Here I am, staying home, baking chicken, and fixin' dinner while the rest go to church." Bitty brought a head of cabbage and a small bag of carrots from the refrigerator and washed them. "I don't mind the cookin'," she shrugged. "I gotta do something, but I can't rightly say it's easy to go to church and hear the pastor read from the Good Book, as your ma would say, and expect everyone to forgive or forget whatever it was that hurt them in life and just move on."

The small appliance whirled, chopping larger slices of cabbage into bite-size pieces, then the carrots and last a small onion and a bell pepper. Bitty poured out the fluid and stirred ranch dressing into the mix. Adding a tablespoon of sugar, she placed clear wrap on top of the bowl and set it in the refrigerator. "Yes sir, she looked like a little angel. That curly hair," Bitty sighed. "Sometimes we don't know which end of her head it grows out of, can hardly get a brush through it. And her tender headed, too."

Happening to glance out the window, she saw the driver of the Suburban using a scraper on the windshield. "Why, that's probably the one Harriet saw. He's pretty short, round too, and wearing that small billed cap she mentioned. Wonder what he's up too. Don't remember anyone in the neighborhood fittin' that description."

"Now it's wait time. Wait for the chicken to cook, until time to put on the potatoes and open those two cans of green beans." Bitty sat down at the kitchen table. "You know, Larry, if things had just been different, we would be gettin' ready to have our own Sunday dinner."

From her chair, she could see the black Suburban pulling onto the street while she sat contemplating what to do next. *I made those two apple pies yesterday.* For a second, as she looked around the kitchen, it was almost as if Larry was speaking to her. *Go get Ellen's Bible and read that Scripture the pastor mentioned last week when he was talking about the innocence of little children and how they often lead the way.*

Well, she didn't know where the passage was found. But Bitty rose out of the chair and retrieved Ellen's grandmother's old Bible. "Just let it fall open, Bitty," that's what Ruthie always said. "And that's our advice."

"Mercy," Bitty said aloud. "I better not tell Ellen, not only do I talk to myself, but today, people are answering." She grinned, opening the Bible. "I won't understand it, but I'll read it." Settling in, she studied the concordance, thumbing through for a word. "Little children," she said as she searched the pages.

———

"He's still there," Ruthie announced in a whisper that carried the length of the aisle. She nodded importantly. "See there, Andy. Baby Jesus is still in waddling clothes."

"Shh." Ellen lay one finger against her lips, as she heard the people on the row behind them chuckle. As the worship hour progressed, Ellen considered Bitty's absence until her mind pressed on to Merelee's death. She hadn't had time to tell Anne. In an effort to bring her attention to the service, she glanced across the aisle. A smile crossed Daniel's face as he nodded and turned to his aunt, who then waved. She supposed he arrived during the time of prayer, when all eyes were closed. She saw his aunt pointing toward the floor; her right foot was wrapped in ACE bandages, and she was using a cane. Ellen gave a sympathetic nod.

"Mommy, Mommy." Ruthie's whisper rang across the room. "Who is that?"

"A friend." Ellen leaned down to whisper in her ear. "Now don't whisper so loud."

"I want to meet him." Ruthie grinned broadly in Daniel's direction. "He can be my friend too." The people on the back row seemed to enjoy Ruthie's enthusiasm.

If an adult could become invisible, Ellen tried. From that time on, she neither glanced right nor left and tried hard to soak up the words the pastor was saying. Had she noticed, Anne was listening to every word while tears ran silently down her face.

"There's no work you can do," the pastor was saying. "You simply believe Jesus came to this earth to be born a virgin birth by the Holy Spirit, lived and died on the cross for our sins, and after dying arose again." He stepped down from the pulpit and walked the aisle, his eyes on the congregation. "You say it is too easy. Surely there is something you must do." He paused. "Salvation comes by grace, not by works, lest any man should boast." He held his Bible up. "What more can you give our Lord this holy season than that? Believe. As the choir sings, simply believe."

"Oh soul are you weary and troubled," the choir began to sing as Ellen saw Anne's shoulders begin to tremble. *Oh, Anne*, she thought, remembering the words to the hymn and singing in a soft voice, "Turn your eyes upon Jesus, look full in His wonderful face and the things of earth will grow slightly dim, in the light of His glory and grace. Oh, soul are you weary and troubled? No light in the darkness you to see, There's a light for a look at the Savior, and life more abundant and free." Harriet with a somber expression was patting Anne's arm.

The choir became silent as the pastor said, "I have an announcement to make before we adjourn. Merelee Fith, as you may have heard, died yesterday in a car accident." He held up his hand as the news settled across the pews. "Merelee was one of our own. John and Mary Fith, her parents, are not with us, understandably, this morning, but they thank you for your prayers. The funeral will be held here at Christ Church on Tuesday at eleven o clock in the morning. Visitation will precede the service, from eight until eleven, for those wishing to attend."

Anne's shoulders were shaking as she turned to pick up Andrew, heading for the door. She broke the line, waiting to take the pastor's hand, and hurried to the car. Ellen hoist Ruthie onto her hip and followed, passing by Daniel with a silent plea for understanding that she did not pause to speak, receiving from him a compassionate nod.

Anne had reached the car and was standing gripping Andy against her breast, a mewing sound was coming from somewhere inside her chest as Andy wiped tears from his mother's face.

"I didn't know," Anne wailed. "I didn't know. I went to school with Merelee. At one time she dated the boy next door to where I lived." Anne tried to wipe her nose, open the car at the same time, and hold on to Andy.

"Here. Let me take Andy," Harriet said as she arrived, taking the child now that the doors were opened and placing him in his car seat.

"Her life was almost as hard as mine." Fresh tears ran down Anne's face, smudging the mascara into streaks that she swiped at frequently. "I had no idea Mr. and Mrs. Fith attended Christ

Church." Gratefully she accepted a tissue Harriet had drawn from her purse. "She has a little boy. He is about seven by now."

"Was she divorced?" Ellen asked.

"No. No, she never married the child's daddy. He was older, and I think he already had a family of his own." The wailing was settling, but the tears continued. "I'm such a mess. I fall apart at the smallest thing, but this isn't small. It's Merelee's gone."

"Better the daddy didn't marry her," Harriet said quietly. "Won't be as hard on the grandparents taking the little boy." Turning to Ellen, she said, "You better drive."

Watching them get out of the car, Bitty could tell something was wrong. She opened the door wide. "What's wrong?" She examined their faces as they filed into the living room. Quietly, she took each coat, hanging them on the rack by the door. The group seemed shut down with not an ounce of energy as they found a seat and sank into it. Motioning for Harriet to join her, they had barely cleared the door between the rooms when Bitty asked, "What has happened?"

"A friend and fellow student was killed yesterday in a car accident," Harriet explained, "and as far as I know, they found out just as worship service was dismissing." She shrugged, "As for the little ones, I guess they are picking up on their mothers' emotions."

"Well," Bitty moved toward Ruthie, sitting in her mother's arms. "I'll change Ruthie into play clothes, and you take care of Andy. We can feed the children, and by then maybe the girls will be ready to eat."

Harriet stood a moment by the window. "Wouldn't you think someone had better things to do than sit in a parking lot all the time? That black vehicle is out there as usual." She let out a huff of air. "Maybe his lady friend, if he has one, kicks him out."

"Maybe he's a courier. I saw him leave earlier, but you mean he's back?"

"Courier?" Harriet asked, looking puzzled.

"You know, delivering things," Bitty offered. "Waiting. Sometimes the UPS trucks park in empty lots to divide their parcels, don't they?"

CHAPTER 12

It was four o'clock when the doorbell rang. Ellen answered to find Daniel standing there. "I thought you might need to retrieve your car," he said.

"Yes, I do," she said, stepping aside, "Come in. Thanks." She pointed to the sofa. "I'm sorry about church. Anne was so upset over hearing Merelee had died." She swept a hand over her brow. "It was so hectic this morning. I didn't have a chance to tell her."

"We were a quiet group, returning from church. It was more like in shock for Anne. Then the children played so hard they were worn out. Now," she sighed, staring off into space, "everyone's asleep, even Bitty." Her eyes met his, explaining, "The lady who keeps Ruthie; she's more like a relative than anything else."

"Which one was she?" Interest sparked in his eyes. "At church, this morning?"

"Oh, Bitty wasn't there." Ellen sank onto the sofa. "Would you like to sit for a moment?"

"Actually, I'm afraid the roads will start freezing again, and I think you should be back home as quickly as possible." He glanced around the room. "Charming," he said. "I like it."

"I'll get my coat." The clock gave its quarter-hour medley. "They will all sleep until we ..." she paused. "I mean until I return, but I need to leave a note for Bitty where I'm going." Stepping to the table, she penned a hurried note. "I'm not sure if Anne has to take Andy back to his father this afternoon." Her voice trailed off. "She has been so upset over a plethora of things lately, I worry about Anne."

He reached across to tilt her head, one gloved finger beneath her chin. "You don't strike me as a worrier."

"Usually I'm not, but Anne's a good friend, and her worries are like a full plate."

The street lights came on to cast a yellow gleam across the snowbound lawns. For a moment, Ellen remembered the night Anne was abducted and shuddered, wondering why that thought would come to her now. They had all agreed to put the incident out of their minds, but it kept surfacing. "It seems night is coming earlier these days."

"It's this weather," he replied, "keeping the evening hours gray and gloomy. Not at all what we want for Christmas, rain and sleet one day, snow the next. No wonder they call this the Show-Me state."

"How did you end up in California?"

"Business. Sprinkler systems and alarm devices." He laughed, "I know, I've heard it before, that's an odd mix. Then you add a little textile on the side to make it all interesting."

"You are blessed."

Driving as carefully as he could, Daniel wanted to study this woman, whose little girl had waved at him, unbeknownst to her mother, during the church service. "You are blessed yourself," he replied. "Your daughter is a delightful little charmer. I truly hoped to meet her."

"She is the light of my life. I think that's why it hit Anne and me so hard hearing about Merelee. Having a little boy, with no father, to leave alone in this world, has made us wonder about our own situations. I don't know what would happen to Ruthie …"

"If something happened to you, you don't know what would happen to Ruthie?" In the dark, he felt her turn toward him. "Wouldn't her father step up to the plate?"

"He hasn't," she sighed. "No, I don't think he would."

"Here we are." He pulled into the mall parking lot. "I can't imagine people out in this weather shopping." He reached for his hat in the backseat. "Before I forget, word has it, they may have to change the plans for Merelee's funeral until after Christmas. Something about a brother in service can't be home until then." He shut the door and came around to the passenger side. Taking her hand he helped her down, a foot on the step, then to the pavement. He brought her close and kissed the top of her hair. "I'm sorry this weekend became one of sadness," he said, drawing her to the warmth of his body, smoothing her hair as one would a child's. "I want nothing but goodness and joy for you."

Ellen felt so tired, weary of all that had happened. "Thank you," she said. "I'm in some sort of spell. Presently everything seems unreal. If I could just sink into the comfort you offer and forget for a while." She gave a feeble laugh. "Ever felt if you let go, you might not find strength to go again?" His arms tightened around her. It was the best comfort she had felt in a long time.

"I have experienced that feeling a time or two in my life," he replied, pushing away to lay hands on her shoulders. "Nothing I'd like more than to hold you forever, but you are on your last leg, and by now Ruthie will be awake wondering where you are."

Sitting in the driver's seat of her own car, Ellen stared up at Daniel. "How did you grow up to be so nice?" She yawned. "I think I'm going to miss you when you return to California."

Leaning forward, Daniel placed his lips on hers, lingering longer than usual. "Hmmm. That was nice." His eyes were the warmest shade of blue. "I will drive home with a smile. Hope you do, too." With a Boy Scout salute, he backed away, laughing. "I'll call you, or you call me. I will follow you home, but I won't come in." He followed, watching as she parked and walked across to the house. He noticed her friend's car was absent from the lot. Shaking his head, he turned around and headed back to his aunt's. They were watching the ballgame tonight.

Throwing caution to the wind, knowing she expected everyone to hang up coats, Ellen laid hers on the back of a chair and sank into the warmth of the sofa. Hadn't she been there before, exhausted to the bone? Before her mind could reply, she sat there savoring Daniel's kiss, not one of passion, but gentleness and caring. And still she had felt a stirring in her heart.

Bitty found her there. "I swear, girl, you have a smile on your lips. Are you asleep?" Looking around expectantly, she said, "Where's Ruthie? Come out, come out, wherever you are, and we will go find some noodles." She tried to sound worried. "Where is that girl? I'm going to cook noodles and finish them off with a cookie. Ramen noodles, Sunday night special," Bitty called, going out of the room.

The usual giggle did not sound. "Ruthie. Give it up." Ellen yawned, stifling the sound behind her hand. "Come on, Sweetums. Bitty is ready for us. You love noodles. You can open the package." She rose, going to the kitchen. "I will pour the milk." Ellen realized just how weary her body felt. "Has she slept all evening?"

Bitty whirled around, her eyes fixed on Ellen's. "What do you mean? Didn't you take her with you?" Worried now, Bitty began to search all of Ruthie's usual hiding places.

"No, I didn't disturb her. She was asleep upstairs when I left. I knew I was coming right back." Seeing the alarm in Bitty's eyes, Ellen ran up the stairs. "What time did Anne leave?"

Bitty was right behind her. "Around four thirty. Andrew called and told her to bring Andy home."

"She has to be hiding, Bitty." Frustrated, Ellen said, "This time I think I'm going to have to spank her. It scares me so badly, when she does this. How else will she ever know? But I'm always so relieved, I just hug her."

———

Easing out of the lot, Garcia glanced down at the roll of covers he had placed on the floor behind the console. He was almost laughing like a maniac, so relieved he had made it down the stairs, out the door, and across to parking. "Right under their noses," he quipped. Once, though, he knew he was running close, when he saw the mother's car coming down the street. But now, he fairly glowed with success. First block he turned right, passed McDonald's, headed east on Kings, cautioning himself silently, *keep it slow, keep it slow.*

All that surveillance planning, hours in the cold, listening to the dames talk had paid off. Garcia French thumped the steering wheel, lightheaded with success. He reached for the cell on the dash, glad he hadn't taken it inside; someone might call. French was no bungler. He had the number on speed dial.

"Cookie is in the oven," he said. There was a pause. "Cookie is in the oven," he repeated.

"Got it." Emphysema coughing came over the phone. "I thought you were going to botch this one, French." There were more hacking coughs. "You know the plan. From this point on, you and that broad you stay with keep it quiet. Hunker down, don't go nowhere. I'll make the call. Come tomorrow, we're in the money." The line went dead.

On Main, Garcia cruised past two patrol cars. City cops, he mused. They got no idea what I'm carrying. "No sir," he spoke aloud. He was mentally rubbing his hands together. "Wonder what the boss is really makin' off this deal. Better still, who's he dealin' with?" He heard the roll of covers stirring, reached behind the seat, and gave a pat to the bundle. Light as a feather, she hadn't awakened at all during the transfer from house to the Suburban. Just one more block … he had to get her in the house before the nosy neighbors got word there was a kid missin'. "Yes sir, you want something done, call French."

The shadows of night hid the way to Onie's front steps. Almost home. French shift the bundle, reached for the door knob.

"What you got there, French?"

A cigarette glowed as Howard, the next door kid, took a draw.

"None of your business, Howie. Go on home."

Howie laughed. "Bet you got Onie a Christmas tree, huh, French? You know that ain't what she wants. What she really wants is …"

"Go home, kid." Garcia slammed the door shut behind him. "Onie," He called. "Onie."

Dressed in wide-leg fuchsia pajamas, the top a spaghetti strap deal falling off her shoulders, Onie came and leaned down to see what Garcia was unwrapping. "Why ain't she purty." Onie sank down on her knees by the old couch where Garcia had laid her. "I wish she was a boy, though."

"Well, she ain't, and we gotta keep her quiet till we unload the goods."

"She's the goods?"

"Yeah. Now what's to eat? I'm starvin'." Garcia stretched, heading for the kitchen. "This work gets kinda nerve wrackin'."

———◆◆———

ELLEN AND BITTY LOOKED BEHIND every piece of furniture, running up the second flight of stairs to the attic. Ruthie was nowhere in sight. Shaking, near collapsing, Ellen ran back down to the kitchen, grabbed up the house phone and dialed Anne's number. Anne answered on the second ring.

"Anne, listen to me, we can't find Ruthie. Do you think she might have gotten in your car to ride to Andy's with you?"

"No. She was asleep on your bed when we left."

"We've looked everywhere. Please, Anne, go look in your car, just in case."

Leaning in to Ellen, Bitty could hear Anne telling Andrew to hold the phone. Ellen could not find Ruthie, and she had to go look in the car ... but she knew Ruthie was asleep on Ellen's bed when she left.

Andy came on the line. "Ellen?"

"Yes."

"I'm sorry to hear this." He had no more than uttered the words before Anne grabbed the phone. "El, she's not in the car. Oh, El, call the police. I'll be there as soon as I can."

"Call the police?" Ellen was dumbstruck. "Bitty, she really isn't here."

"No." Bitty could say no more. She stood there, terror-stricken. "I'll go check all the places again."

Ellen was dialing. "Will we have to go to the police station, Bitty?"

"No, I believe they will come here."

The two detectives came, parking in Ellen's ice-encrusted drive, their car sliding to a halt. They barely waited for it to stop before jumping out and hurrying toward the door.

"Mrs. Anderson?" Recognition dawned in the cop's eyes. "I thought this address sounded familiar. "News came over the radio," he paused. "Your little girl is missing." The two were stomping snow off their shoes. "I'm Officer Cullens and Officer Ben Hankins," the larger of the two said.

"Yes. Yes. Come in." Ellen was wringing her hands in agony.

Bitty watched the two give each other a brief nod. She could only wonder what they had already decided. "Sit, if you wish," she said, a bit curt. Ellen had already lowered herself carefully onto the big chair where her coat was lying.

"Mrs. Anderson, were you the last person to see your child?"

"Yes." Ellen shook her head. "No, I left with someone to go to the mall to get my car. My friend, Anne, said she saw Ruthie asleep on my bed when she left to take her son back to his father." Ellen's words died off to a whisper. "He lives across town."

"May we speak to your friend …" He paused. "Anne?"

"She's on her way back."

"Is there a possibility your daughter might have gotten in your friend's car?"

"No. No. I called her and asked."

"How old is your daughter?"

"Three." Tears streamed down Ellen's face as she remembered Ruthie always said she felt like four.

"We have to make a complete report, Mrs. Anderson; the quicker we get the information out, the quicker we will find your daughter."

"I understand," Ellen whispered. She felt stone cold inside, and her hands would not stop shaking.

"Is there anyone else you should contact … your child's father, perhaps?"

"No, he doesn't care."

"He is the biological father, isn't he?" the smaller one asked. "He has rights."

Bitty placed a scrutinizing stare on Officer Hankins until he fidgeted where he was standing to slide uncomfortably into the straight-backed kitchen chair she had placed in the doorway.

"We need your husband's name," Cullens said, "where he lives and phone number."

"Ex-husband." A sob caught in Ellen's throat. "Florida. He moves around a lot." She was faintly aware Bitty was placing a blanket around her shoulders. "I no longer have his phone number; anyway, he doesn't answer." Guilt and grief were waging a war within her mind, and they wanted her to think about Jeffrey.

The door opened. Harriet stood there, contemplating the scene. "Bitty, what's wrong?" The police officers appeared to turn with words, whether of warning or comfort, Bitty couldn't tell, but Harriet held up one hand. "I don't need your information; I merely ask my friend, what's wrong?"

"Ruthie is missing."

Harriet clasped one hand over her mouth, hurrying to Ellen's side.

"And you are?" Officer Cullen asked.

"That's none of your business," Harriet snapped. "I'm a neighbor."

"Then you might as well know," Officer Cullen replied, "you and anyone near this house will have to answer a lot of questions in order for us to find this little girl."

Harriet stiffened, but thought better of a snarky reply. "For Ruthie, I'll unload my diary," she stated. "Now Bitty, when did you first miss Ruthie?" She glanced quickly toward Ellen, shaking beneath the blanket. "She's gone into shock, if I don't miss my guess. And where is Anne?" Regaining curiosity concerning the presence of the police car in the yard, Harriet began to ask all the questions the police officers needed to ask, bit by bit piecing together the information they needed to make a report.

"I can tell you this," she said finally, addressing the two. "You take care how you handle this. No bungling information that would cast blame on any one of these ladies that lives here, or I'll see that your heads roll."

Cullens stiffened, standing suddenly to his feet. "Ma'am, do you know it's a misdemeanor to threaten a police officer?"

"I'm not threatening you," Harriet replied. "Your captain is an old friend of mine. You want to tell him what I said. Be sure to tell him who I am. Harriet Becker."

"Of Becker Iron Works?" Cullens asked, blanching.

"The same." She cast a stern glance their way. "Yes, sir, that's right." Harriet met Cullens' question with her arms crossed and folded tight across her chest. "Don't you think you better send word to your captain to put out an AMBER Alert?"

The police report was on the radio within the hour, although an immediate check of cars had evolved in the first thirty minutes of the officer's arrival with road blocks set up at every entry to the city. Neighborhood watch began, unmindful of weather and icy conditions. Neighbors Ellen had never met showed up with flashlights in gloved hands, wearing hooded shirts and heavy coats against the freezing temperatures.

"What are they doing?" Bitty asked.

"Canvassing the neighborhood. They will go all the way uptown, at least a two-mile radius, I'd say," Harriet replied as she stood near the kitchen window watching the whole procedure. "It's good, the neighbor's turning out."

"You were a little scary talkin' to those police officers," Bitty whispered, glancing carefully to where Ellen stood staring out the front windows. "She wanted to go, but they told her to stay here in case someone calls."

"Well, I was scared out of my mind when you said Ruthie was missing. I still am, but Ellen looks bad, Bitty. Real bad."

"You really know the police chief?"

"Yes, I do. I wouldn't lie about that. I don't know if he will remember me; it's been a few years," she sighed. "I just wasn't myself; maybe I will have to apologize to those two, but at least it got them going."

CHAPTER 13

"You really think you should go back out on those roads tonight?" Andrew stomped across the floor to the window and threw back the curtain, looking out onto the iced street. "It's treacherous. Even I won't drive under those conditions."

"I have to." Anne's voice came soft and low, between bouts of tears.

"You just got here. There's nothing you can do." He glanced across to where their son lay sleeping on the sofa. "You should have taken him in to his bed. Now if he wakens, he will be up all night."

"What is wrong with you, Andrew?" He was acting stranger than usual.

"What is wrong with you?" he mimicked. "I let you keep Andy on my weekend," he stared up at the ceiling, "and you are so ungrateful. Now just because little Ruthie is missing, you want to go right back over those dangerous roads to help Ellen find her. She's probably hiding behind the couch. They'll find her."

Anne kissed Andy's cheek and started toward the door, struggling into her coat. "I can't believe you are so coldhearted you don't care about a little girl that is missing. If it were Andy, would you be any different?" Slinging her purse over her shoulder, she stared at him, her mouth a hard narrow line. "You've always been cruel, Andrew, but this ... this is the worst."

"I just wanted you to stay."

"Why? Because your girlfriend dumped you and went home to her parents?" Agitated, Anne opened the door as he came bounding toward her, his arm above hers, pushing the door shut while her hand was still on the knob. She felt his breath hot on her neck, as she remembered—this was where he usually hit her, but this time she was leaving.

"Let me go. You call your girlfriend and put your mighty body against hers. You hit me this time, Andrew ... I swear I will call the police." She pushed back, catching him off guard, struggling for balance as his hand latched onto hers. He was stronger. Laughing, a wicked sound, he spun her away from the door, turned the lock, and slammed her into the nearest chair.

"You're not going out on those roads." He was bending over her, his nose nearly touching hers. "You are not going anywhere." Gaining composure, he straightened, wearing his *I am in control* face, speaking as though nothing had happened. "I want to talk to you." He shrugged. "You can spend the night."

"Spend the night? You normally can't get rid of me quick enough. Do you think I believe you have enough goodness left toward me to let me spend the night, when for months you've dogged me on everything from where we will be to the exact moment you want him back home? I've allowed it, because I felt I had no choice. You fixed everything, didn't you, Andrew? With your high paying job, your choir boy reputation, except it's not quite so pure, is it ... did your little princess find out you aren't the prize you claim to be?"

"Shut up." Andrew drew back a fist. "Haven't you learned yet?"

One knee shot out as Anne pushed off the chair. "Have I learned?" Anne's body trembled, remembering, but she couldn't stop the torrent of words, locked in her mind all these months.

"You won't hit me this time, Andrew." Her breathing was ragged as she glanced toward Andy, wondering how he could possible sleep through their fighting. "You always made me think I wasn't as good as anyone else because of my family." With one hand, Anne smeared away the tears. "Well, you are finally free to take your bullying somewhere else; I plan to build a good life, for now for myself and our son, and who knows, maybe someday a good man will come along."

Andrew's laughter rang loud in the room. "You are damaged goods, babe, who do you think would want you? Haven't you got it yet?"

She was gaining control as she spoke softer, "You need to take a good look in the mirror, Andrew. Do you like what you see?"

"What I see is a woman that never appreciated me."

"That's not true. But you wanted to be worshiped even when you did wrong. I loved you. And until this afternoon, I thought I still did, but it has ended. In a way, it makes me sad because I thought Andy deserved his parents together, and even though you were with another woman, I could forgive you and take you back ... but I think you revealed yourself completely when you had no compassion for Ellen. You should be ashamed. She took me in when you threw me out." Gaining courage, she edged toward the door.

"I didn't throw you out." He sank against the chair. "She threw me over this weekend. I wanted to ask you what you thought. I just wanted to talk. It made me mad; you didn't have time for me."

"She threw you over ... who? For what?" Surprise overshadowed her anger as Anne finally understood. "This is about your girlfriend. She left you?"

"For her old boyfriend. Yeah," he nodded. "They are at her parents. Together."

Anne stared at him, unbelieving. "You would ask me?"

"There was a time we could talk."

Incredulous light dawned in Anne's eyes. "I'm the wrong person to discuss your girlfriend with, Andrew. What we had was supposed to be a marriage. And what we received from it was a wonderful little boy, a gift from God."

"What do you know about God?" He smirked, his eyes cruel.

"Not half as much as I intend to know," Anne replied. "I'm changing, Andrew. With God's help, I want the best life He has to give me. People fail you, but I don't believe He will." It seemed an eternity; the two stared at each other, and she wondered that he remained still. By some miracle, she might leave without a broken bone this time. Quietly she opened the door and left. Passing Andrew's shiny BMW, she got into the old Chevrolet and backed out of the drive. She had cleared Rondale Drive at the end of Andrew's street when she saw the car above, on the overpass, being pushed over the rail by an eighteen-wheeler. "Jesus save me," she whispered, as the air around her was filled with the crushing sound of metal against metal and her world went black.

The sound reverberated through the streets. A block away, Andrew thought he felt the foundation of his home move. Rushing to the door, he could see an accident at the end of the lane. Beneath the city lights, an old tan car sat squashed with a newer bright blue molded onto its top. "Anne," he screamed. "Anne."

Doors opened as people stepped out into the street.

"Second time that's happened," someone said. "Both times, snow and ice on the overpass."

"Andrew, you all right?" His next door neighbor was peering up into his face.

"Mrs. Peterson, could you spend the night looking after Andy. I think he will sleep through the night." Andrew gulped for air. "I think that's his mother's car."

A sea of emotion flooded through Andrew's thoughts, all because he had treated Anne so badly when he had a taste of her misery himself. At last, he understood. It was her last words that cut him to the bone in his hours of despair; hadn't he wondered if there was a better way? She said she found it. He didn't know what she meant. A gnawing in his gut told him he might never know.

They stood staring down the street. "It's not good, Andrew," Mrs. Peterson said. "Of course I will stay with Andy if you need to go to the hospital, and in the morning we will go back to my house. Don't worry about your child."

Static sounded on the police radios Cullens and Hankins wore on their shoulder. The two officers had returned from the group canvassing the neighborhood to say they had not found the little girl. "You want to get that?" Hankins asked Cullens as the static continued. With a nod Cullen left them, going to the police car.

"I'm sorry, ma'am," Hankins said to Ellen. "You are welcome to come to the station, but it's probably best you stay here in case there's a call for ransom."

"Ransom?" Ellen's face paled, as her shoulders sagged. "I ... I ... I'll stay here." She felt, rather than saw, Cullens' return to his partner's side. Though he spoke quietly, Ellen heard bits of the conversation: "Older tan Chevrolet," and "Rondale Drive." Her mind scattered, trying to assimilate the information.

"Anne's son's father lives on Rondale Drive," she said aloud. "Anne drives an old tan Chevrolet." Unaware of her actions, Ellen's hands were on Officer Hanken's arm. "*Is* it Anne?" she demanded. "Tell me, is Anne all right? She was coming here."

Officer Hankins was trying to release the death grip she had on him.

Ma'am, I cannot divulge police information."

"It is Anne, isn't it?" Ellen gulped for air. "How bad is it?" She walked behind Officer Cullens as he was returning to the police car.

He was speaking into the microphone. When the button released, they heard, "An ambulance has been issued to Rondale Drive and Exit 5 at the overpass on Interstate …"

"Where will they take her?" Ellen gripped the officers' arms, one hand on each man's sleeved arm, demanding, "Is she alive; which hospital will they take her to?"

"Ma'am." Hankins tried to loosen her hold. "I cannot give you police information."

The radio crackled with static, and then the words came across the air. "The patient is trapped inside the lower vehicle. Paramedics are working with the patient as the life team cuts through. She will be taken to Cox Medical Facility to stabilize, depending on the extent of her injuries, and in the event it is deemed necessary, airlifted on to St. John's Mercy."

Ellen backed away from the police car, bent double, arms clasped around her body as she swayed drunkenly toward the porch. Bitty and Harriet came, wrapping their arms around her back, supporting Ellen as they led her up the steps into the house.

A second and third police car pulled in front of the house. One man hurried inside, going straight to the phone; a second stopped by the women, flashing a badge. He said, "I am Captain Chester Mayfield. I will be here, along with Officer Officer Miller, in case a call comes through. Your phone is being wired to go through to our main headquarters." They were a huddled and subdued group as they heard but gave no reply.

"Tell us, Ellen," Bitty whispered. "About Anne, it's bad, isn't it?"

"Yes." Ellen sank onto the sofa, the two sitting on either side of her, waiting. "It's not just Ruthie. Anne has had an accident.

They're cutting her free of the vehicle." She doubled forward as the phone rang. "I think I'm going to vomit."

Bitty had retrieved the phone as Harriet dashed to the kitchen for the waste paper can. "Ellen, it's some man," Bitty said. "He says it's about Ruthie."

Wiping phlegm from her mouth, Ellen took the phone from Bitty.

"Have you found her?" Ellen clung to the receiver. "Please, I'll come get her. Just tell me where you found her."

"Listen carefully. Place one hundred thousand dollars in a plastic bag, put the bag inside a five-gallon gas can, and leave it behind the Dumpster at Belton's Cleaners and Hope's Beautifying Salon. You know where they are located?"

Ellen nodded, soundless.

"Lady, do you know where Belton's is located on South Main?"

Again, she nodded.

"Speak up. You want to see your little girl again?"

A sound evolved from Ellen's lips.

"If you call the cops, you won't get your child back. You understand?"

"Yes," Ellen struggled to keep the vomit from spewing into the phone. "Yes."

"Repeat my instructions," the voice said. "Now."

"Place one hundred thousand dollars in a plastic bag, put the bag inside a five-gallon gas can, and leave it behind the Dumpster at Belton's Cleaners on South Main, and don't call the police." Sweat had broken out on Ellen's brow; her skin felt cold. She had no strength left; the phone dangled in her hand as Bitty wrapped her fingers around Ellen's.

"Right." A hacking cough interrupted his next words. "Tomorrow morning, six o'clock."

"I don't have one hundred thousand dollars," Ellen wailed.

"That's your problem," the voice replied.

"Please. You have to give me more time to see if I can borrow the money." She knew she had nothing on which to borrow, but she had to plead for time. "Please don't hurt her."

"That's your call." The line went dead.

"Did you get that?" Harriet turned to the man who had been working on the phone earlier. "I suppose you are getting a voice tape, aren't you?"

"They are using some type of metallic device that distorts the voice. We will have to run it through, but there is definitely some type of cough going on in the caller. Did you hear that, miss?" He turned to Ellen, a sympathetic expression in his eyes as she leaned across the waste paper can again.

THE PHONE RANG AS THEY were sitting down to dinner. James answered, an apologetic expression in his eyes. "Sorry, hon," he said to Salena. "If it's Ray about that boat he wants to buy, I'll tell him I'll call him back." Lifting the receiver, he said, "Hello."

"Is this the Lewis residence? James and Salena Lewis?"

"Yes. This is James."

"Do you have a paper and pencil, sir? I believe you should jot down this number."

Puzzled, James reached for the pad by the phone that held a pen as well.

"Mr. Lewis, forgive my interrupting your day and your lives, but I believe it would profit you and the missus to call your daughter."

"Hold on a minute, how do you know my daughter?"

"Oh," the voice said. "I know your daughter and that sweet little granddaughter too."

"We don't have a granddaughter," James clipped, starting to hang up the phone, but he heard the man continue speaking. "What did you say?"

"You should call this number, sir. I believe it will be most enlightening." The line went dead, accented by a hacking cough the caller could not suppress.

"That was strange." James returned to the table, scratching his head, thinking. "It was a man said he knew our daughter and granddaughter as well. He gave me this number, said we should call them."

"Do you think it is some kid making a prank call?"

"If it is, the kid has emphysema," James replied. "I don't know what to think of this. You say grace, hon; I'm a bit unsettled over that call."

The prayer of thanksgiving finished, Salena stared across the table. "Who would do such a thing, especially when we want Ellen back in our lives so much?"

——— ———

"Least you and I know about each other, the better," the boss said as he hacked a few times.

""You have a terrible cough," the man replied. You say pickup is tomorrow morning, six o'clock. I don't know … you think that is feasible? Can she get the money?"

"I called that other number to sweeten the pot."

"What did they say?"

"Didn't have no granddaughter."

"Yeah, they'd say that. But you can bet your last dollar, when it hits home they may indeed have a grandchild, that's when the bank opens."

"It better or we got one three-year-old girl someone has to deal with. Now don't let the money get away, and whoever has the little girl, tell them not to hurt her."

"Now you care," the man grunted. "Late thinking, ain't it, on your part."

You know nothing about me," the boss replied. "Just get the money. Remove your part, and leave the child in a safe place. You got that straight? Safe."

"I got her a safe place all right, and she will be returned to momma as soon as we have the dough. Right?"

"You know where to leave it, and no staking out the drop off." The boss hung up.

The man didn't like that cold resolute voice that said a million different things, each meaning the boss thought he was better than anyone he ever dealt with. Who did he think he was to say no staking out the drop off. Of course there would be surveillance overnight. A million cops couldn't keep that from happening. He wasn't in this business for nothing. Little girls taken from family were especially rewarding. He had to laugh. What would the boss say if he knew he had hired another person to handle the girl? He would see to the money swap, but for now he couldn't be hampered by a child.

CHAPTER 14

Captain Mayfield asked Harriet and Bitty if he could join them. He needed information. "We can sit there at the kitchen table. I sense you ladies support each other." His associate, Officer Miller, took out a notepad and pen. "Officer Miller will keep notes of what we say, Mrs. Anderson. I understand you have no contact information on your child's father, his whereabouts, or his phone number?"

"No, sir."

"Then let us jump to the other information." Raising his head, he met Ellen's eyes. "Have you had your daughter fingerprinted at any time since birth?"

"No, sir."

"Have you heard of the AMBER stick that can be uploaded in PDF format, containing DNA?"

"Yes, sir, we have studied that in our nurse training. But I have not done it with Ruthie."

"Do you know anyone that would kidnap your child for any reason, gratification of having a child, to hold for ransom, or to coerce you into compliance on a personal matter?"

"I don't understand."

"Is there anyone who stands to benefit in regard to kidnapping your child? Is the father of your child of that nature?"

"No, sir, I don't believe that about Jeffrey."

Captain Mayfield sighed. "Have you at any time searched for registered sex offenders near your neighborhood?"

"I thought sex offenders have to register, if they live within a specified distance of a child?" A troubled expression settled on Ellen's face. "Is that what you are thinking?"

"Mrs. Anderson, there are always those who do not register, or those who have never been caught. I have to ask these questions."

Ellen's heart raced; she thought it would jump out of her skin. She felt deathly sick, heartsick. She had failed Ruthie in the most horrible ways. Were they truly asking questions required for finding a missing child, or did they think Ruthie was already dead?

Trying to zone in on their questions and remember at the same time what she had studied in class, she was sweating profusely while her hands were numb and cold to the touch. "Forty-seven percent of children abducted are murdered within the first three hours," she said dully.

Nodding, Captain Mayfield sighed and asked, "What is your relationship with your husband, and what is his with the daughter you share?"

"Obviously there is no relationship if I don't know where he is, and it seems plain that he does not care how his daughter's life is going. He is an ex-husband."

"Do you have parents, Mrs. Anderson?"

"Yes." She fought the tears that dared to surface.

"How often are you in touch with your parents?"

"Not often."

"Would your parents be capable of taking your child?"

Swallowing hard, Ellen forced a reply. "They do not know I've had Ruthie."

"You feel your parents are not aware you gave birth three years ago to a little girl?"

"No. They don't know, and if they did, they are good people. They would never take Ruthie away from me."

"What if someone wanted to gain money in exchange for your daughter? Would your parents pay?"

"You mean ransom?" In her heart, Ellen realized if her parents had known Ruthie, they would pay.

She said, "They would, but they don't have that kind of money."

Nodding at Officer Miller, Captain Mayfield stood. "Run a check on Mrs. Anderson's husband. You have his date of birth and last known state of residence. Do the same with her parents. By now, Cullens will have the data on every known sex offender within a fifty-mile radius, starting right here on the hill, and see if the roadblocks have turned up anything. Jed has probably arrived at the station by now. When he arrives he will turn the dogs loose and let them sniff out anything around Mrs. Anderson's home."

Stretching, the captain motioned for Ellen to follow him. "We need several pieces of your daughter's clothing, Mrs. Anderson, preferably something that she may have worn that has not yet gone through the laundry."

Hearing the captain's request, Bitty pointed to Ruthie's small play coat on one of the pegs by the door. "I can get her tennis shoes in the basement, if you want. I took them down to clean, but I haven't gotten to them."

"That would be a good start," Captain Mayfield nodded. "Now, ladies, if we might continue.

"Ms. Bitty, you are the one who watched Ruthie every day, right? And Ms. Harriet, you are the next door neighbor?" He noted both in agreement. "Now, ladies, let us do a general breakdown of what this neighborhood experiences on a day-to-day basis. If you remember a stranger in your neighborhood lately, tell me. Or, if someone you see on a regular basis seems to have been acting strangely, tell me."

"It's almost nine o'clock," Bitty said as they finished their discussion with the captain. "Do you mind if we turn on the television to hear the report on Ruthie?"

"No. Go right ahead. If you don't mind, I'll make another pot of coffee. We are in for a long night." He was already emptying grounds and rinsing the pot. "I noticed you had the coffee sitting right here, or I wouldn't have been so bold in asking."

"Breaking news. The three year old we reported missing earlier has not, at this time, been found. We are informed police blocked all entries into and out of our city. A canvas of the neighborhood in which three-year-old Ruthie Anderson lives has turned up nothing, and even now as experienced canine groups are in the community, there is no news forthcoming. You, our listening audience in the Channel 12 area, are asked to notify the authorities if you see or hear any news pertaining to this case.

"There was an accident at the intersection of Rondale and Exit 5 to Interstate 55 tonight when an eighteen-wheeler lost control on ice-slick roads and careened into a blue Nissan Sentra, pushing the Nissan over the rail to land on the South bound lane of Rondale Drive on top of a 1989 Chevrolet. The two cars became embedded, and the driver of the Chevrolet is in serious condition in Cox Medical Center waiting airlift to St. John's Mercy. The airlift has been delayed due to thick fog in the area, an unusual occurrence with snow and ice covering the ground. Elsewhere ..."

"Oh, dear God," Harriet moaned. "Anne's car was crushed to the door. How could anyone survive that?" She pulled a tissue from one pants pocket and dabbed at her eyes. "Bitty, don't you think we better go to the hospital?"

"What about Ellen?" They stood staring at Ellen, sitting on the sofa, holding Ruthie's coat and shoes.

"Ma'am." The captain's voice interrupted their thoughts. "You can't drive in this fog, but if you feel you must go, my men will take you to the hospital and stay with you until you are ready to return." Taking a sip of coffee, he continued. "Officer Miller and I will be here with Mrs. Anderson."

"What should we do, Ellen?" Harriet asked, dropping down by Ellen's knees, placing her hands on Ellen's.

"Go for me. I need to know how she is. Say a prayer, so Anne will know God is listening. And I will pray here."

It was past midnight when Harriet and Bitty tip-toed into Anne's room. The hospital was stone quiet. Anne lay on pressed white sheets, her small body barely denting the creases. A huge bandage wrapped around her head, a patch over one eye, Anne's bruises were less seen but perhaps more evident.

"Her pelvic bone was broken, she received a blow to her kidneys, and both ankles are fractured, no doubt all due to her body crushed downward when the heavier vehicle landed on top of the car she was driving," the nurse explained. "There is some internal bleeding … the doctors are not certain where it is coming from, maybe no more than the pressure various organs suffered during the delay in cutting her free of the metal and debris at the scene of accident."

"Is she in a coma?" Bitty asked.

"According to Dr. Blaine, your friend's body suffered such trauma, they thought an induced coma would allow her to rest before the aftermath of what happened set in." She finished checking the small machine by Anne's bedside. "The tubes will remain until all is well. The doctors will decide in the morning if your friend is to be transferred to St. John's Mercy." Patting Bitty's hand, the nurse left the room.

"Ellen said we must pray," Bitty reminded Harriet. "You will have to … I can't."

Harriet sighed. "Why don't we call Ellen?" Picking up the receiver by Anne's bed, Harriet dialed. "They won't like this, but it's important." She waited for the ringing to stop and heard Ellen's voice come over the line. "Ellen, neither Bitty nor I know what to say; actually we can't pray. I'll lay the phone by Anne's ear, so she can hear you."

They knew Ellen would be wondering what to do if a call came through from the person who had taken Ruthie. Still, her voice came, praying for Anne. "Father in heaven, we need you now. Please watch over Anne in the hospital, and if it's in your plan, let her remain here, near Andy. Lord, we cry out to you from the depths of our hearts, heal Anne's body; comfort her in waking, Father, that her thoughts rest in you and not in what has happened. Strengthen us all, Lord, in what we now face and what we face in the future. We place our lives in your hands, dear Lord, knowing you have given us permission to ask in our time of need, knowing you hear us, you are there. Now, Father, we pray thy mercy on our lives. Bless Anne, as only you can, heal her according to your will, and Lord, we give you praise now and always, in your blessed holy name. Amen."

They heard a click of the line. The connection was broken.

"We ask too much of Ellen," Bitty said. "I think it is all right for us to leave now."

Outside, in the hall, adjacent to Anne's room, a young man was sitting. Seeing Bitty and Harriet, he arose and came forward. "Are you friends of Anne's?"

Harriet nodded. "We are. I am Harriet Becker. This is Beatrice Shaw."

"Andrew Graves," he offered his hand. "Anne and I were married. We have a son. You may know …" He stumbled for words. "It's a long story. I'm afraid I am the bad person in this story."

"Why are you here?" Not one to hold back, Harriet questioned, her eyes dark with foreboding as she assessed Anne's former husband. "Anne has mentioned you."

"Forgive me," Andrew searched for words, "I'm not sure why I'm here. It's difficult. Seeing her lying there like that; they said her blood pressure won't stabilize, that someone should be here." For a moment it was as if some great tremor ran through his body.

"Anne is a good person. I'm not." A tangle of unintended words seemed to rush out. "She said I broke her spirit, until today." His eyes held a strange expression. "I don't know why I'm telling you this. It's like I have to, for her sake, for mine." As a child might do, he thrust his hand against his mouth, pressing hard until his knuckles turned white. "It's like I have this horrible fear. I don't have anyone here to be with me. I thought Ellen would come, until I remembered, about Ruthie ... has she found Ruthie?"

"No. The police are still looking."

"Ellen possesses some kind of rare insight." There was an unnatural parlor to Andrew's face. "It's like she can makes sense out of the most unreasonable circumstance. I saw her influence on Anne, and I envied Anne knowing her. When she would tell me things Ellen said, I ridiculed Anne and railed against her friend, but later I always realized Ellen had some inside view of life that saw things from a different angle. I never admitted this to Anne." He gazed at them, searching.

"It was like I wanted to hurt Anne. I didn't care. It took my mind off my own failures. I see Anne changing in front of my eyes these days, and I don't like it; she says she wants the peace and security Ellen has. How is that? Her troubles are a mile long, and yet she has given Anne some kind of hope. I can't understand what Ellen has that we don't."

"Ellen knows God," Harriet replied softly. She was prepared to dislike Anne's husband. He had not been good to Anne; therefore she would dismiss him from her mind, in fact from the human race, but here he stood needing to pour out his plethora of sins to she who was little better, she who could not pray. "Whether you or I believe in God, Ellen Anderson does. God forbid the worst should happen and Ruthie not be returned, Ellen will survive because she believes in God."

"Anne does too," he said. "She told me tonight. I never saw Anne that strong before. She stood up to me." Shame faced, he admitted, "I challenged her. In my own disappointment, I tried again to beat her down with words of ridicule, just like before, when we were married."

"Why would you do that when you let her go? As I understand, you divorced Anne. You are planning a life with someone else; why would you mistreat Anne?"

"Because I could." He bowed his head, almost cringing, "There's something in me has to ..." Shame seemed to overcome him. "I don't know why I'm telling you this. I don't even know you. And I don't know Ellen. Evidently she has something Anne wants."

"I told you," Harriet replied, a kindness she was wont to recognize toward Anne's ex-husband. "Ellen knows God. Anne is searching for Him, through his son, Jesus."

"I think she found him," Andrew said. "She seemed so different."

As they settled into the back seat of the police car, Harriet whispered, "I can't believe I almost felt sorry for Anne's young man. I kept reminding myself about the bruises you saw and his mean-spirited way of treating her concerning their son." She sighed tiredly. "Ellen would have had her Bible out, leading him in the plan of salvation, and here I am, I couldn't even pray."

"You did all right." Bitty patted Harriet's arm. "I am so mired down with thinking about Ruthie, I can't seem to go beyond all that has happened tonight. It's the worst I've ever seen. Ruthie is missing. Anne in an accident, and my heart aches over Ellen. The whole time I've been trying to pray within me for everyone. I don't really know how anymore." Bitty raised a handkerchief to her eyes and dabbed. "I just feel so guilty not attending church with all of you, like it's my fault Ruthie is missing. It's just about more than I can bear." For a time, they rode in silence, each in their own thoughts.

"Lord have mercy," Harriet exclaimed seeing the clock on the car's instrument panel. "Two o'clock in the morning. No wonder we are worn thin." She leaned forward, "Officer Cullens, is there any word on Ruthie. Has anyone called?"

"No, ma'am." Cullens pulled the car into the lot across from Ellen's house. The drive was blocked. "Ladies, wait. Let me help you across the street."

Harriet glanced around the lot. "Well, at least the courier is gone, if that's what he really was."

Cullens' hearing picked up. "What do you mean, *courier*? As in one who delivers something?" Taking a lady on each side, he began to walk them toward the house. "Did either of you mention that information to the captain?"

"What am I going to do?" Ellen demanded. "The hours are passing. Six o'clock will be here, and the bank won't open until nine. What must I do?"

The captain exchanged a glance with his associate. "It is a hard thing you face, Mrs. Anderson. We thought another call would come in."

"But who?" The strain of waiting and not knowing what to do had taken its toll on Ellen. Silently, with Harriet and Bitty gone, the other two speaking in hushed voices, she had prayed, asking God to protect Ruthie from the evil surrounding her and to answer the prayers of the people.

Once the news aired, the pastor from Christ Church had come, surrounded by many from his congregation. While he spoke with Ellen, a vigil in Ruthie's behalf was taking place in the yard. At midnight, strains of music, in *a cappella*, rang softly through the neighborhood. By two o'clock, many of the weary returned to their homes, while others remained holding candles in glass jars to lighten the dark.

Anxiety in her voice, Ellen called to Bitty and Harriet as they came through the door followed by Cullens, the officer. "Did you see Anne?" Her heart ached all the more seeing the expression on their faces. "Oh, she is alive, isn't she?"

"Yes. Yes." The two rushed in to sit beside her on the sofa, leaning in to see each other's face. "She is so pale on those white sheets, and Andrew is there. They said someone needs to stay."

"She is that badly hurt?"

"Something about her blood pressure will not stabilize. There are tubes running out of her body, here and there," Harriet spoke in short sentences, remembering. "Broken pelvis, something concerning the ankles they are not certain if fractured or broken. They are keeping her sedated due to the trauma of the accident, something about her reliving it."

"You both looked so sad, I feared the worst when you came through the door."

"That was because we remembered something," Bitty sighed, wrapping her arms around her body. "Whether there is a coincidence or not, there was an old van and a black Suburban in the lot across the street the last week or two. We neither one mentioned it to the captain, but Cullens says it may be important."

"I don't understand; how could that be important?"

Shrugging Bitty said, "We don't know, but the same man drove both vehicles, and Anne was certain whoever picked her up was in an old van of some sort. I think they will have a few questions for Andrew."

"But Andrew would have no reason to take Ruthie."

CHAPTER 15

"Time is ticking away," the captain said. "I don't know about the rest of you, but I'm beginning to think this is an inside job or at the least has to do with family. Mrs. Anderson doesn't know where her ex- lives. Her friend was abducted earlier by someone in an old van, but due to bad weather and circumstance, no police report was made." His eyes narrowed on the two officers. "Now a child is missing. If it is family, they won't hurt the child, but the middle person or persons has no loyalty to anyone; therein is the problem. If someone gets scared or feels threatened, what will they do with the little girl?"

"Dump her," Officer Miller said. "I worked cases on child abduction before." Weary, she rubbed her forehead, thinking before continuing. "In this temperature, outside, she wouldn't last long, and if there's a place they think she won't be found, that's where they will leave her." She handed over a dozen papers to the captain. "I think you wanted this info."

He thumbed through, stopping at one. "Call Mrs. Anderson's parents. Now. I want them here ASAP." To the officers, he said, "Go to the hospital, talk with Mr. Graves." His eyes narrowed in thinking. "Ask him if he has an alibi for yesterday evening. He is going to need someone to vouch for his whereabouts."

"Miz Harriet," he said, joining the three in the living room. "Do I remember you?" A slight smile played on his lips. "It's been a decade, hasn't it, since you straightened me out over a game of cards."

Smiling, Harriet rose to offer her hand. "Captain, I wondered if you would remember."

"I remember all right, but when a child goes missing, I admit everything else clears the mind." He sighed. Motioning for her to sit, he pulled the straight chair closer. "Now tell me what you know about this mystery man, a Suburban, and an old van. The captain listened, interested in their stories of seeing the van and its driver.

"Gathering the bits and pieces you have given me," he said after they finished, "it appeared to you that this man was waiting for someone." They nodded. "Did it ever occur to you that he might be spying on the house?" Seeing Ellen blanch, he asked, "Mrs. Anderson, do you need the waste basket, again?"

"No, sir," she replied weakly "There's nothing left inside of me to throw up ... I feel so guilty that I thought we were all safe, when it's possible someone was right under our nose intending to do us harm."

"We have to move fast in the morning, Mrs. Anderson. By six o'clock, I will have contacted the bank where you do business. It is my hope that the middle man will be getting anxious, wishing he had set a later hour for pickup when he realizes there are no banks open in this town on Sunday, and he is going to have to lengthen the time for you to get the money together."

"All I have is this house I bought with money my grandmother left me. I don't think they will lend me that much on this old house."

"So much of this is trial and error," the captain replied. "Every case is different. You never know how to play it. For now, we are putting an APB out on the description of the driver of the old van." Seeing Bitty's puzzled expression, he explained, "An all-points bulletin."

Readying herself mentally to speak with the president of the bank, Ellen realized it would be far easier to throw herself at his feet, so dire was her need for Ruthie's ransom. How had she come to this? Her daughter missing, a call demanding money ... and she stood looking into a mirrored image of a very pale young woman she scarcely recognized. At some hour between midnight and now, they impressed upon her the need to sleep. How could she sleep when her arms were empty, her child missing?

"Mrs. Anderson?" The woman they called Officer Miller stood outside her bedroom door. "There is a gentleman here, a Mr. Daniel Bates, says he must speak to you."

Her breath caught. It was true, in the midst of the turmoil and fear for Ruthie's safety, she had thought of him, as yesterday's events unraveled. What would a man think of a woman losing her three-year-old child? Minute by minute, her own guilt battered at the very core of her heart. She knew the facts according to child molestation or kidnapping; within three hours' time, usually the victim was dead. But she had prayed throughout the night, praying Ruthie was asleep and unaware of where she was or whom she was with. She had asked God to wrap her child in the safety only He could provide and to soften the hearts of those who had taken her.

"Mrs. Anderson?"

"Yes, I heard you." Collecting her purse, coat, and the papers to her home, she followed down the stairs.

He met her as she stood on the last tread, staring into her eyes, his own clouded with concern. "Why didn't you call me?"

She only shook her head, speechless.

"We didn't have the television on, to hear, until this morning," he said. "I came immediately."

Taking her hand, he led her into the adjoining hall for privacy. "What can I do? I took the liberty of speaking with the captain. He brought me up to date with what has been done. I know the city outlets are blocked; I was stopped on the way over." Taking her coat and the papers, he laid them on a table. "And he said the feds are on it." His hands covered hers, rubbing gently. "You're hands are cold as ice."

"I feel cold inside. Sometimes I find myself shaking so hard I can't control it."

Pulling her closer, he bent to kiss the top of her hair. "The captain said you are ready to go to the bank. May I accompany you? He thinks the call will come shortly, and I want to be with you."

Ellen glanced around; beyond the hall where they stood, the same people held command in the kitchen, although they seemed either to have gone home to change uniforms or somehow freshened the rumpled uniforms they wore at midnight. Bitty was busy serving coffee as usual, and Harriet was absent.

As she opened the envelope with the house papers, she was aware the doorbell rang and someone entered the house, followed by whispered conversation, but she was unprepared for Bitty's hand on her arm.

"Ellen, I think you better come see these people."

GARCIA FRENCH WAS IN AN agitated state, each step punctuate by a hiss of denial, as he bounced across the floor. "What do they mean?" Sputtering, he stood hands on hips, now staring into the face of the television commentator, "All entries to the city have road blocks; all citizens are asked to comply with inspection of their vehicle." He turned to stare at Onie.

"Who do they think they are, asking regular citizens to comply?"

"Ain't nothin' regular about you, Garcia," Onie said. "I'd say you are about as *unregular* as they come." She grinned, showing teeth ravaged by the use of drugs.

Garcia flexed a muscle, strutting importantly in front of his girl, until the worry returned. "I'm supposed to be ready to take the kid to the boss as soon as the mommy drops the dough. She's to stash it in a gas can behind the cleaners and Hope's Beautifying Salon, where he will pick it up and I'll leave the kid."

"But, Garcia, Hope's is closed on Mondays and so is the cleaners. Timmy will get cold outside. Besides, how you gonna know when she leaves the money?"

"Hello?" Garcia pointed to where his cell lay on the table. Eyes narrowed, he asked, "Who's Timmy?" Garcia leaned across Onie, threatening, "I told you her name's not Timmy. She ain't no boy, Onie. Get that outta your head."

"I'll call her Timmy if I want," Onie shouted, pouting. "And you ain't droppin' her or him out in the cold."

Garcia shook his head, figuring. Onie had taken a shine to the kid; maybe in that warped mind of hers, someway connecting this kid's presence to that boy she gave away. He couldn't remember what she had called her boy, probably didn't remember herself what she named him. Already, he knew he had trouble with her on his hands.

"Onie, hon, let's don't do nothin' to mess up this deal we got goin'."

"You got goin', you mean," she sulked. She was taking in the details of kidnapping as the guy on the television explained, "Following the Lindbergh kidnapping, the United States Congress adopted a federal kidnapping statute allowing federal law intervention, which is necessary if the kidnappers cross state lines. In some states, if the victim is harmed in any manner, it becomes a crime for capital punishment."

"What's capital punishment?"

Garcia slapped both hands against his head. "Punishment by death, you dope head."

"That's it." Onie leapt up from the chair. "I've had enough of your macho-whatso. Who do you think you are, Garcia French? Einstein?"

She gave a hollow laugh. "We'll see who's so smart." She sprang from the room. Slamming the door shut to her bedroom, she locked it and moved toward the child on the bed.

Garcia moved toward the telephone and stopped. Outside, that Howie from next door was at the window, trying to see inside the house.

"Must'a heard the report," Garcia mumbled. "Now I got more business to take care of." Grabbing his shirt, he pushed his arms through the sleeves, retrieved the cell phone, and stuck it in his pocket."

"You behave now, Onie. I gotta take care of Howie."

Outside, Garcia covered the distance, hooking one finger in Howie's coat collar.

"I know you got something in there, Garcia," Howie yelped as Garcia's nails dug into the back of his neck. "You let me go, or I'll turn you in."

"For what? Bringing in a bundle of clothes to wash?"

Opening the bottom drawer, Onie removed a set of clothing from the chest. Every year since she gave Timmy to the authorities and signed the papers adopting him to a good home, Onie had bought new clothes, trying to chart her son's growth.

"All right, Timmy, it's time to run. Now you just sleep on." Taking a small bottle from her purse, Onie pressed a pill inside the child's lips. "I will change your clothes and we will get out on the road in no time. Garcia French can put that in his pipe and smoke it." Taking the scissors from the top of the dresser, "First things first," Onie said as she began to cut the curly locks from Ruthie's hair. "You are gonna be a right handsome boy."

Within minutes, Onie had packed her own overnight case, dressing in a warmer jogging suit, bright purple with rabbit fur collar, and pulled on knee-high boots. She dipped one hand down into the bed post, satisfied when she counted the two fifties, three twenties and a one-hundred dollar bill. She had her own little business on the side. What Garcia French didn't know didn't hurt him. A girl had to save up for times like these. She almost laughed. Wouldn't he be surprised when she cranked up the old Nova? She had made a believer out of Garcia, saying she'd lost the keys, and the car had been reported as salvaged, anyway, and couldn't be driven.

One of her regular customers worked as a mechanic. While Garcia was away, her mechanic had worked on the old Nova and said it ran smooth as a whistle.

She heard Garcia berating the kid next door. She liked Howie. Sometimes they shared a joint, and while she didn't want Timmy growing up like Howie, he wasn't a bad kid. Drawing in a deep breath, she slung her purse over one shoulder, laying Timmy in the curve of her arm and the keys and case in the other hand. She was ready. Peering out the window, she saw Garcia knocking on Howie's parent's door. Good, he was stepping inside, no doubt to remind the parents they were doing a miserable job raising their son.

Driving out the back, Onie flipped a finger Garcia French's direction, wondering how long until he realized she was gone. She knew a way through the alleys to avoid the road blocks. At the end of Blaine and Grant, old man Tollison's farm allowed her a means to access the interstate. Maybe she was taking a chance, driving the interstate, but who could find fault with a mother and her son headed home.

Glancing back, Onie smiled. That sleeping pill she put in Timmy's mouth had dissolved by now. He would sleep all the way.

Following Bitty, Daniel watched as Ellen' demeanor changed from sadness to an indescribable hesitation to move farther into the room. Had the situation not been so somber and heartbreaking with Ruthie missing, he would have thought for a moment that Ellen's hesitation bordered on joy, but it was immediately replaced by a frozen countenance. It seemed her body bowed and her feet would not advance, as her head drooped to her chest.

"Ellen." The woman came forward, followed by the man. Daniel judged them to be in their fifties. The woman was smaller than Ellen, but there was a resemblance.

"Mom?" Ellen sagged as the woman's arms closed around her body. The father moved in, his arms wrapped around the two. "Oh, Mom, my baby's gone."

"We know." It was a heart wrenching moment. There were tears in all their eyes, and Daniel closed his tight, thinking sadness is hard to look on.

The father struggled to gain control, his hand resting lightly on Ellen's back. "We didn't come to interfere. We just want to be near you and help if we can."

"Dad." Ellen turned into her father's arms. "I've missed you both so much." Her body shook with pain. "Daddy, it's so hard."

Dan didn't see a dry eye. The two officers, standing by the door, cleared their throats and headed outside. The captain seemed to be heaving a sigh of relief. Dan guessed he had sent for the parents, unbeknownst to Ellen.

"Mrs. Anderson, it is time to go to the bank."

"Yes." She struggled for composure. "Mom, Dad, come with us." Her eyes were luminous as she turned, taking Dan's hand, to introduce them. "Dan is coming with us." Dan nodded, shaking her father's hand. There was no time for conversation.

"They didn't seem so bad," Harriet whispered to Bitty. "What's that all about?"

Bitty's mouth narrowed to a straight line. "I don't know the whole of it, but it had something to do with Ellen's husband. I can't talk about Ellen, Harriet." Clearing the kitchen table of dirty cups, she said, "That girl got no sleep last night. I could hear her praying, sometimes just the whispered movement of her lips." Bitty sighed. "I don't know if mine got past the ceiling, but I did too."

"You didn't rest either, did you?" Harriet eyed her friend with compassion. "Why don't you go lie down? Let me clean up this mess."

"No. I can't rest until I see Ruthie again."

"That's a large amount of money," Ridgeway Montgomery said. "Your home as collateral simply won't meet the requirements."

"It's all I have." Ellen's head fell to her chest. "Please think of a way."

"Ellen, we can help if we have time." Her father glanced at the police chief. "Do we have time to draw our money out of annuities?"

"No, sir, the time is set, six o'clock. And it is now fifteen till."

Daniel stooped down by Ellen's knees, peering into her face. "May I?" One finger beneath her chin, he raised Ellen's bowed head to meet his eyes. "Will you let me do this for you and Ruthie?"

"It will take me forever to repay you," she whispered, tears running down her cheeks.

The money was dropped at precisely six o'clock. The gas can was shoved between the trash cans behind the cleaners and Hope's Beautifying Salon. Both were closed, but there was no sign of the little girl.

"Something has gone wrong." Officer Miller relayed the news by cell to her captain. She was staked out a short distance from the cleaners. "Maybe they got word the police were informed." She watched a kid sliding off his bicycle, squatting on the ground as he realigned a detached chain. A few minutes later, he rode off.

"Move away," the captain said. "Maybe they are suspicious, with you sitting on the street."

The guys from the Federal Bureau of Investigation had arrived in time for the drop. Armed, one was inside Hope's, the other at the cleaners. From windows that viewed the trash cans, they waited as the officer dressed as Ellen placed the money.

At Ellen's home, the ringing of the phone brought the huddled group to life.

"Hello." Her voice was a strained whisper.

"You want to see your little girl again?"

"Yes. Yes."

"Tell those officers and those two inside the buildings to move away." Coughing came across the line. "Did you really think the place would not be under surveillance through the night?" More coughing sounded in Ellen's ears. "Now, we want everyone in clear view. Tell them take a drive down to the nearest McDonald's."

"Where's Ruthie?" Ellen was desperate, her hands shaking, and she was hardly able to speak.

"I will let you know when our business concludes."

Garcia was in hot water. He had missed the boss's call. "Where were you, French? I called you to bring the kid." A bout of coughing interrupted his speech.

"They've brought the police in. I knew they would. But the money is there. Soon as they move away, I'll pick up the money for you." Garcia was stretching the truth and grasping for a straw, but he had his own contact. He told the kid from the street, "Watch what goes down. Ride your bicycle. Call me; let me know what you see." He had tried to cover all areas, and still he was in hot water. Maybe he picked the wrong kid.

"You listenin', French? Your job is the girl. Remember?"

"Yes, sir," Garcia swallowed, hard. "I had a kid tryin' to peek in the windows I had to take care of. That's where I was." Sweat broke out on Garcia's brow. The boss wasn't listening. He had his own agenda.

"Listen up, French. I'm going to overlook that ... this time. After all, you got her, all safe and sound. Right?" The hacking cough started up. "Soon as they leave, soon as I got the dough, I call you; you drop the kid at the McD on Rand Street, across town. You can go down the alleys, avoid the road blocks, see? Is the kid smart enough to walk across the street?"

"I don't know."

"It's your problem, French. It's just part of earnin' your money. Stay tuned. I'll be callin' you pretty quick. Keep the kid safe." The line went dead, Garcia listening to the boss coughing.

"Onie," he beat on the bedroom door. "Open up."

She didn't reply. With his ear against the door, his blood pressure soared as Garcia listened for movement. "Onie, open this door or I'll kick it in."

From the local television station, thought to be the highest spot for surveillance, one of the city's own was watching through binoculars. "He is headed for the alleys, moving toward Main and Seventh. Now, I can't see him. Someone better close in or we are going to lose him."

"You hear that, Captain? Contact has been broken. He has disappeared."

CHAPTER 16

Miller arrived back at the Anderson home, personal defeat written all over her face. "They lost him," she said quietly. "He disappeared."

"No trace?" The captain walked outside, disappointment and frustration claiming him. So much was riding on the drop executed, the child received in exchange.

"The feds thought they had him, but he disappeared?" Staring at Officer Miller, he was bitterly trying to put the pieces together. "Only one way he could vanish, he went down a pot hole. Call the water department, ask them if there's an underground network on Main and Seventh." He silently berated himself.

"I mentioned this to the feds, but they said it's their show here on out. I'm to mind my own jurisdiction, and they'll let me receive all the glory." His teeth were set on edge. "It's not glory I want. It's the little girl."

—◆—

Hitching his pants, Garcia stepped back, rushed the door, lifting one foot to kick it in, and fell panting on to the footboard of the bed. "You drugged out …" His words stopped midair. The room was empty. Onie was gone, and so was the kid. A pile of hair lay in ringlets on the bed covers. The morning news rang fresh in Garcia's head. *In some states, kidnapping is a crime punishable by death.* Garcia French dragged himself back into the living room, sinking on the ratty old couch. What was he to do? Run? Or wait it out? The boss had the money. Who was going to rail about a missing kid if they had the money? What did the kid have to do with anything? He had to think. He wasn't smart enough to pull this off by himself. Good thing the boss hadn't caught his words. He would have asked, "How do you know the money has been dropped?" No sir, the boss wasn't so smart either. *But I'm the one sweatin', and Onie has the girl.* Someway, he had to get himself out of this mess.

GRIM FACED, THE CAPTAIN RETURNED from outside where he had tried to clear his head of the defeat and disappointment. The money was gone, but the child was not returned. It was almost more than he could bear. They were all watching him, expecting good news.

"Captain?" Ellen stepped forward.

The remainder of his life, the captain would remember the hope in her eyes, the pasty white of her skin … and he knew that hope would diminish and quickly turn to despair while he lingered, trying to form the words of denial.

"They didn't get your child, Mrs. Anderson."

Daniel caught her as she folded. He heard others speaking and was aware of emotions surfacing as he placed Ellen on the sofa that everyone had cleared. Ellen's mother sank by her daughter's side. Disappointment claimed them all; the room had become deathly quiet. Bitty and Harriet found themselves clinging to each other.

It was as near an acceptance of defeat as any group could suffer. Straightening, taking it all in, Daniel stared hard at the captain.

"What do we do next?"

"They have the money."

The captain pulled a handkerchief from his back pocket. Wiping sweat from his brow, the big man's shoulders drooped as he pushed the piece of cloth back into the pocket and glanced apologetically around the room. "All we can do is wait and see if they drop the child some other place we would least expect." Gripping the back of the chair in front of him, the captain said quietly, "If ever there is a time to pray, I suggest you do it now."

Daniel stepped into the hall to take out his phone and dial his aunt's number. "Aunt Georgia. They were unable to bring Ellen's little girl home. She's still out there somewhere. I think you need to call your church, inform the pastor, and get the prayer groups focused on this."

He listened as his aunt reminded him, "God works in mysterious, son, His wonders to behold. You tell Ellen not to give up."

What could be mysterious about kidnapping an innocent little child, demanding money, and then not leaving her? What it was, was evil, and his hands were tied. If God would work a miracle, that's what it was going to take. He replaced the cell at the moment Ellen's father came, motioning to him.

"Son, would you be so kind as to help me take Ellen upstairs. It's like the life has drained out of her. Bitty tells me there's a chair; you can sit by her bedside."

"I will, but you and your wife might want that privilege."

"No, son, right now, me and Sally have some strong praying to do, and these ladies who have been with Ellen all along promised to fill us in on all that's happened. What Ellen needs is to rest. We don't know how long this situation will play out."

Together, Daniel and Ellen's father carried her up the stairs where Daniel kept vigil, listening to the ticking of a bedside clock and the rhythm of her breathing. The ordeal of Ruthie's abduction had worn her to the bone. At times, she became so quiet Daniel would hold his breath, waiting, encouraging her silently, and relieved when she stirred. Her mother had pulled a quilt around Ellen's shoulders, kissing her daughter's cheek before leaving the room. He heard a scrape of a kitchen chair against the floor, the opening and shutting of the front door. It reminded him of the quiet of a house when someone died.

A shudder went through his body. If there were something he could do ... but the captain encouraged them, one and all, to wait, not let their imagination run wild nor give up hope. Still, there was no plan of recourse. The AMBER Alerts were out to bordering states. Ruthie's photograph was flashing in major cities on billboards that usually carried advertisements. Daniel had seen the look in both the captain's eyes and his partner, Miller. It had long passed the three-hour recovery for expecting a kidnapped child to be alive. By now the kidnappers would be panicking, trying to destroy evidence, and Ruthie was the evidence.

"Daniel?"

He was standing at the window, watching cars pass on the street below, when he heard her call his name. Turning, he came to sink down beside her, reaching for her hand. Their fingers entwined, as she said, "I'm sorry to involve you in ... this."

Kissing her fingers, he replied, "I wouldn't have it any other way."

"But you hardly know me, and you haven't met Ruthie at all." Tears pooled in her eyes, spilling over onto her cheeks. "I'm overwhelmed by your kindness, and while my greatest concern is for Ruthie's ... safe ... return, I am aware of the loss of your money." A sob hung in her throat. "I don't know what to do, Daniel, and here I am talking to you ... when you don't know me and I am lost in this ... this battle; it's the hardest thing I've ever faced."

"I'm sorry." Sitting up, she pressed the quilt against her face, hiding while fresh tears flowed, as the quilt became wet and her shoulders shook.

"Maybe we know each other better than you think, Ellen." His voice came softly, as though he must be certain each word was exactly right before it was spoken. "On another occasion, I remember searching for something to fill a void in my heart, someone or something to carry me through a very rough time. My heart ached for understanding. I wasn't sure I could live through it."

She remembered he had spoken of being hurt. "Was it when Madonna broke your engagement?"

He gave a hollow sort of laugh. "No. That hurt my pride, but now I know it was God's blessing. I've been saved a life time of pouting demands from a spoiled young woman used to having her own way." He sighed. "It was when my parents died together in the wreck. I was young, and even though I knew they had a lot of problems, it did not matter; they were still Mom and Dad. When they were gone, it wasn't the problems I remembered, it was their love. The loss of their love, even at that young age, nearly took me down. I remembered the way my mother twined her arms around me and whispered in my ear. She would say, 'Do you know how much I love you?' and I would always ask, 'How much?' I thought my dad was the strongest and smartest man in the world. I didn't really understand their adult problems, I only knew what they were to me ... and the loss was terrible."

"What did you miss most?"

"Ballgames. The other kids had parents rooting for them. Parent-teacher night, my parents were absent, and I learned just how important it is for a kid to have someone of their own present. I missed my dad, with his arms around me, holding the bat just so, and encouraging me. It wasn't just one thing; it was many." He sighed. "I was a kid. Nothing seemed fair."

"How did you ... I don't know," she said softly. "How did you compensate?"

"I lied to myself sometimes. And to others," he grinned. "Aunt Georgia and Uncle Bill were usually there, and I'd think the other kids don't know they aren't my parents." His grin widened. "There appears to be some kind of shame a kid suffers if everyone else' parents are there and theirs aren't. Don't ask me to explain that."

"I'm sorry."

"Don't be. In a while I became so used to Aunt Georgia and Uncle Bill being there I forgot to lie, even to myself. I still missed my mom and dad, but I was beginning to realize how much they loved me. They suffered through every miserable stage of my boyhood, and Aunt Georgia is still standing in my corner rooting me on." He squeezed her hand. "Not all children are that lucky. As I grew older, I began to see kids my own age whose parents didn't seem to care, and sometimes those kids fell by the wayside."

"Do you think Ruthie is alive, Daniel?" Brutal pain registered in her eyes.

"What do you feel in your heart?"

"That she is alive." She picked at the quilt where a loose thread appeared. "You know that verse, Trust in the Lord, with all your heart? I don't think I was asleep, but when the captain said they were unable to ... they did not have Ruthie, it was like I was dying inside. I wanted to escape from it all, if just for a moment feel nothing, and God gave me that verse." Swallowing hard, Ellen continued. "I falter, Daniel. I believe, but I have such a fear they will hurt her. Then that Scripture comes back to my mind. I don't know what to think. I close my eyes and try to send Ruthie a message."

"Just keep trusting, Ellen. I wish I could say more. All I know is, people are praying, and God answers prayers. It is your job to trust in the Lord, no matter what happens." He sighed. "It is not always easy."

———

ONIE CRAWLED OUT OF THE car, examining the ruts. The car had settled into an indescribable depth of mud. She knew exactly the moment it fishtailed and hit bottom.

"Almost there," she said to Timmy, strapped into the back seat. *Almost there* could have been five miles or fifty. She climbed back in, put the car in reverse, and slammed her foot on the accelerator; the car rocked. Quickly she pushed the lever forward, pressing heavily on the gas, laughing crazily as the car advanced a few feet. Again and again, she spun forward until the mud seemed to grab all four wheels, and the vehicle refused to move another inch. She stepped out and carefully to one side; mud was halfway up the hub caps, but she could be proud of the distance she'd managed. Now there was nothing to do but walk.

"Mr. Tollison lives just up the lane, Timmy. Why, he's an old man now." Gathering her purse, the case, and Timmy in her arms, Onie started walking toward the farmhouse. "Lord, have mercy, I thought you'd be light as a feather, but you have grown into a strap of a boy, Timmy."

Glancing at the *No Trespassing* signs, she said, "That don't mean us. Why, I knew Mr. Tollison when I was a kid. My daddy worked on his farm, and my momma cleaned his house when Mrs. Tollison died. I suspect he's a rich old coot by now." She switched Timmy to her other hip, changed out the purse and case in her hand, and tried to walk on. "I swear this must be clay soil, the way it's clinging to my boots. It's going to ruin them for sure." Scrutinizing Timmy, her eyes narrowed as she shook him. "You better wake up now. I saw you open your eyes when we were in the car. Much more of this and you're going to have to walk. You hear? Wake up."

She passed another sign. *No Trespassing.* For a minute she stopped, swapping Timmy and the purse and case again. "Who'd want to? Old goat. I hope he don't have them old dogs he used to keep. Yippin' and yappin' at your feet, slobberin' all over you like they wanted to eat you up. Many a time, when momma and daddy was gone all night, I'd come up here to see Mr. Tollison, and I had to put up with them dogs. 'You go on back home now,' Mr. Tollison would say. 'Ain't right a child your age out at night.'"

Onie huffed, trying to get her breath. "I won't leave you again, but you sure are heavy. You gotta walk." She set the child on the ground, watching as he buckled to his feet. "Wake up. You hear me. Wake up. Don't you sleep no more. All right, then, I'll drag you."

The dogs were setting up a howl. Frank Tollison went to the window. "Probably a stray cat," he said. "Or maybe a possum. You'd think they'd be braver than that. Beagles. Nose to the ground, all the time. Not like the Rottweilers I used to keep."

There was nothing on the highway in front of his house to cause the ruckus. He peered down the lane. Only a fool would take that route, when the ground had been saturated with ice and snow for weeks now. The man he rented his farm to was none too pleased when someone tried coming down the turn row, said it made ruts they had to work all season smoothing out. "You just call the police next time, Mr. Tollison. Just because your farm runs along the city streets don't give people the right to come on your property. I've put up no trespassing signs, but I'm going to Florida for a while this winter, and I won't be here to pull them out."

Back inside, Frank stared through the window once more. "Yes sir, there's a vehicle down there just far enough in, stuck good and no way out. And I don't see anyone near it." Shaking his head, he turned toward the telephone. "I sure do hate to do this, but someone's going to need that car. I guess the police will have it pulled out by one of those fancy wreckers."

A SUBDUED GROUP SAT STARING out the windows. The captain agonized over it all. There had been no word. The money had been picked up. The person retrieving the money had vanished, and no word had been forthcoming on the little girl. His nerves were strung tighter than they had been in years. He had sent Miller back to the office and told her to find a few hours' sleep when she finished the report of the last nine hours. He needed to go home himself, not so much for creature comforts, but to clear his head.

There had to be something they were missing. Piecing together the previous week's activities had been like the old saying, pulling hens' teeth. By the time the women remembered the presence of the old van, the black Suburban, and the man they thought was a courier, the money had been placed, picked up, and still no clue as to who was behind the kidnapping.

Mrs. Anderson's husband supposedly lived in Florida, whereabouts unknown, and there was no way to trace him if he wasn't plugged in to the workforce. The arrival of the young woman's parents had not revealed any new piece of evidence. It had been his opinion, if they were of any substance at all, they would be the first ones tapped for ransom of the child. His mind lingered on the black Suburban. Something tingled there, evading solidity, but it was a gut feeling. When he asked if anyone thought to write down the license, they had met him with puzzled stares.

Except the gentleman who had arrived this morning spoke up. "I actually did write it down," he had replied, "but when nothing came of it I dismissed it from my mind."

Now the captain was groping at straws as his people were running the first numbers Gates remembered. Asked why he could remember that, Gates replied, "Because it was the date of my mother's birth, March nineteen sixty-one."

'Your mother would be fifty-three?'

"Yes, sir," Gates replied. "I wish I could remember the rest. Seems like I want to say *Agnus*, but that's too many letters."

The captain found himself rethinking their conversation word for word. "And why were you concerned with the Suburban?"

"I thought it strange the Suburban followed Ellen home and parked in the lot." He seemed to the captain a nice young man, but he checked his credentials anyway. He was a businessman from California. There were no records against his name.

Sighing, he walked back and forth, across the room, out the door, returning to repeat the same steps. Finally he decided he would go home for a period of time. It was then his phone rang. The group listened intently. Disappointed, they realized a personal call had reached the captain.

"Frank? Yes, I am kind of busy at the moment. Did you say could I stop by?" His breath came wearily. "No, sir, I can't, but I will send someone out." Shaking his head, he waited. "Yes, I'll hold on." To the group he said, "Someone's at his door." He wondered why he felt it polite to explain. "All right, Frank. I'll see what I can do."

Blowing air through his teeth, he closed his eyes to rest. It was just more than he could handle at the moment. He had grandchildren. He wanted to find this little girl as much as if she were his own.

"Sorry about that. I don't know how that call came in. Nothing or no one is supposed to get through, if they aren't connected to this case." He picked up his cap.

"Well, it was my neighbor. He has about the nearest outlet a man could have to the interstate, by way of his farm. I guess someone didn't like our road blocks and thought to go through, but there's no foundation to farm roads after all this weather."

"Frank wasn't as concerned when it was a woman and child at his door. Still, someone has to get the car out of his field. "I'll just step out and handle this."

He had no more left their presence than Officer Miller returned. "I sent him packing," she said. "The man is dead on his feet. I told him I will man the phone, and he is only a call away." She settled in the straight-backed chair. "He told me a personal call came through. Everyone at the station is wired, waiting to jump on any new evidence." Shaking her head she said, "It gets crazy. Probably someone thought Mr. Tollison had news when he asked to speak to the captain. We can't take any chances."

"There have been no calls from whoever took Ruthie?" Sally asked.

"No, ma'am."

"We have never met our granddaughter," Sally said to no one in particular.

CHAPTER 17

STANDING ON THE OUTER FRINGE of Frank Tollison's farm, the captain viewed the ruts left by the old Chevy Nova, some two hundred feet from the street. The driver had probably left the alley, crossed Madison, and thought to take the field road to the interstate. He was surprised the driver made it that far. Erosion had cut away the turn row, runoffs of melted snow still obvious.

Sometimes he wondered at the mentality of people wanting to avoid notice by the law. The plates were out of date. He'd run them anyway, in hopes of finding the owner. He scratched his head. Something just didn't feel right.

Returning to the police car, he opened the trunk and pulled out a pair of insulated rubber boots that he kept for times like these, along with an old pair of Carhartt coveralls he sometimes wore around the house when he made repairs. He changed out of his shoes and donned the coveralls covering up his uniform and badge. It wouldn't hurt him to take a stroll. His mind was so full of the kidnapping, his body suffered from all the tension. He felt like a coiled spring ready to break.

He walked along the side of the field, mushy as all get out, his feet sinking into the slush. In the distance he heard Frank's beagles baying, a sound deep in their throats. Something caused him to keep on going, even after he passed the car. One set of steps, then a drag on the ground reminded him of the days when he was a kid and pulled a sack across frozen ground, snapping bolls from cotton stalks. No one did that anymore. Mechanical pickers took care of the crop, start to finish. Besides, this was no cotton field. The fringe of cut bean stalks was obvious in the snow. He was intrigued. What would a person drag across a turn row to make those tracks in the mud?

Arriving at the house, he stooped, petting the beagles that licked his hand and ran between his feet, making his climb up the steps cumbersome. Knocking on the door, he waited, hearing voices as Frank came to answer.

"Chet. Come in here, fellow." Frank's voice boomed welcome. "Never thought I'd see you after we talked. Come in out of the cold." Scrubbing his feet on the bristled floor mat, the captain stepped inside Frank's house.

"Didn't mean to disturb you, Frank, but I was wondering ..." He glanced up in surprise as a young woman came from the back room carrying a crying child.

"I want to go home. I want my mommy." The child's cries were so agonizing that both men leaned forward in concern.

"This here is Onie Smutts," Frank offered, his attention staying on the crying child. "He ain't happy, that one," he said. "He's been cryin' ever since Onie walked up here."

"You two know each other then?"

"Yes, we do. Onie's pap used to work for me, and her momma helped Christine."

"I want my mommy," the child wailed "Please let me go home."

Something tugged at Chester Mayfield's heart. He thought about the child everyone was searching for, away from her mother, and here was this little boy crying while his mother stood watching. The boy's sobbing overtook whatever it was Frank was saying.

"Come to me," Chester found himself offering. He opened his arms and waited as the boy crossed the room. It was then he noticed the whole backsides of the child's clothes were wet, and there were traces of mud splattered on his face. Chester tried to conceal the hard set of his jaw.

"Ma'am, why are this child's clothes wet?" He knew without a doubt a lie was forthcoming.

"Why, he fell down," Onie replied. "Just fell face down, and I couldn't catch him." She stooped down and held out her arms. "Come to Momma, Timmy."

The child melted into Chester's body, his cries tormented and uncontrollable, as he shook with fear. Without a thought, Chester whispered into the boy's ear. "Is that your mommy?"

"No," he sobbed. "Please take me home. I want to go home."

The mother was clearly irritated. She grabbed up a small boy's coat and slung a purse over her shoulder, all the while glaring at the child. "We have to leave, Mr. Tollison. I can't abide this boy behaving like this."

"Ma'am?" Chester drew himself to his full six-foot-four height. "Is that your car at the end of Frank's field?" He held tightly to the child's hand as he stood there.

Stunned, Onie glanced from one man to the other. "What business is that of yours? I done explained to Mr. Tollison, I am sorry I messed up his road. I will pay whatever it takes to fix it." Reaching down to grab the boy's hand, she pulled, trying to loosen Chester's hold on her son.

"Ma'am, if the boy fell on his face, what reason would there be that the back of his clothes are sodden?"

"What's sodden?"

Chester glanced down with surprise as the child spoke. "It means very wet," he said.

"What did you say, ma'am?"

"Timmy, you shut up," she threatened. "Don't you say another word, you hear me?" Her eyes glaring with hate, she turned on Chester. "For the last time, mister. It ain't none of your business whether he fell on his face or his back. He's my kid, and we're getting out of here." With maniac force, she ripped Timmy free from the captain, jerked the door open, and would have left, except the captain moved, blocking her way out, his hand against the door.

"I'm afraid I am going to have to arrest you on trespassing."

"Hold on here, now, Chester. I don't believe that's necessary, seeing as how I know Onie."

"You called me, Frank." The captain stared hard at his old friend and neighbor.

"Let me get this straight," Onie smirked. "You think you can do a citizen's arrest when Mr. Tollison won't press charges."

"No, that ain't right either, Onie."

Frank Tollison was clearly flabbergasted. "This whole thing has gotten out of hand."

"You're right on that," Onie declared. One hand on Timmy, the other on the knob, she jerked the door again, stopped by the captain's foot.

"Ma'am, I'm calling a police car. And I'm taking you in on child abuse now. If I'm not mistaken, you dragged this child through the mud and snow. That's why his clothes are wet. Family services has a division called CPS, Children's Protection Services. They will meet us at the station." Adrenalin pumped through Chester's veins. "I'm truly sorry, Frank, but there's more going on here than meets the eye."

Apologetic, Frank reached out to Onie. "I'm sorry, young lady. I know we can come out of this with a better understanding …" His words drifted away as his attention fixed on Chester pushing the old Carhartts down to reveal the badge on the front of his police jacket. Here he was trying to bring comfort of sorts to Onie, and the captain, his neighbor, arresting her because she supposedly dragged the boy through the field, and the boy clearly was wet. Frank sank down into the nearest chair. He felt real bad.

In a matter of minutes, Captain Chester Mayfield had radioed his officers. A second car was detached to examine Onie's vehicle, run the outdated plates for ownership, and be towed from the property. All the while, the woman ranted and raved, clutching her son fiercely to her body. If it hadn't been for her language, if she had shown any sign of remorse or tenderness to the boy, perhaps he would have relented. The gut feeling remained. What he was supposed to gain from this encounter, he wasn't sure, but the more he observed the woman, something seemed off-kilter. Either she was running from her family with the child or hiding something. The thought did occur, she was possibly mentally ill. CPS would know.

"Ah, Chester," Frank asked, once Onie was seated in the police car. "I've been thinking this over. Why would you bring family services into this?"

The captain's face was grim. "Frank, no mother drags a child through the mud in such weather conditions. What if there are other circumstance? Children's Protection Services is set up to look into these things. They will check the records to see if there have been other incidents, find out if by chance the mother is running from the father with the child." Chester sighed, "And find out if this mother is stable, mentally and emotionally, to care for Timmy."

"Well, there is that," Frank agreed. "I guess you can call me if need be."

Back at headquarters, sinking heavily into his chair, Chester closed his eyes for a moment. His body had felt near collapse until the boy had come into his arms back at Tollison's. Something about a child's need, he mused wearily, railed against human comfort and spurred the mind on.

It appeared Onie Smutts had no family to call to care for the boy. As he sat thinking, she was being questioned, and from what he observed through the one-way glass window to the investigation room, she was giving his officers a run for it. His thoughts flitted from one situation to another, reliving the last twenty-four hours. Except for a twist of fate, he feared the worst for the Anderson child.

When the money disappeared, and the child was not left, who then had the child, and what would they do with her? He could picture the scene he left at the Anderson home, the young mother visibly shaken to the point of being ill but devoid of accusation toward anyone, while this one was making a stir heard throughout the whole building.

By the language that came out of her mouth, he doubted that one had ever attended church, while the Anderson home, during his hours there, appeared bathed in prayer.

He shouldn't make comparisons, but it was his habit to let his mind settle to roam the alleys and avenues of what he saw, what he felt, and the possibilities of each case.

Whether to press charges remained to be seen. If the child was abducted by a family member, detained overnight, or not taken more than fifty miles, it was one thing. If a child was held for ransom, as in the case of Ruthie Anderson, it became another.

He recalled the two boys found in St. Louis. They were not brothers, and while one had been missing four years, the other was found in less than a week. He prayed that was the case with Ruthie Anderson. Here he sat, pondering why he had felt it necessary to have Onie Smutts and her child brought in … for the welfare of a child and his own peace of mind, he guessed.

Officer Guiles tapping on the window brought him around. He motioned him in. "She says she has a boyfriend, and we finally know the home address. You want us to check it out?"

"Not only check it out—if he has a vehicle, run the plates."

Garcia French chewed his knuckles, a habit formed when he was agitated as a child, usually after he'd suffered another beating from his mother's boyfriends. He packed his clothes, along with the blanket and the girl's clothing Onie had left behind. Showered and dressed in his best white shirt, pinstriped suit, and black felt hat, Garcia examined his appearance in Onie's old dresser mirror. He looked like any business man.

The question was, how was he going to get his share of the dough without turning the kid over to the boss? If his plan worked, he would be down the road before the boss noticed the kid was missing, but if the plan failed, he was toast.

He felt the cell vibrate in his shirt pocket. "French, this ain't good. Get over here, fast."

"Yes, sir." He gave a fake laugh. "You got it counted out?"

He heard the click as a landline went dead. Connection broken, he thought. Better not be. He planned to collect his share and head for Louisiana. His Suburban was vacuumed, scrubbed clean … no evidence to be found.

Roadblocks were still in place. Garcia waited patiently while they examined the Suburban.

"Where you headed?" they asked.

Garcia smiled, his eyes lighting with the milk of human kindness. "Home to Louisiana for the holidays."

They nodded. "Be careful."

Across town, he met the boss in the designated place. Wearing the hairpiece and geek glasses, the man eyed him suspiciously. "Where's the kid?"

"In the truck." Garcia stared back, his eyes slits, insolence on his face, a bluff he wasn't feeling, but he had to push himself through this one.

"Where you parked?"

"Out back. You want I go get her?"

"Send her in."

"That's a little tricky, ain't it?"

"Not for daddy waiting for his little girl, is it?"

"Let's see what you got," Garcia replied. Taking a gift wrapped box from a bag on the floor, the boss lifted the lid, smiled happily for any onlookers to see, and placed the lid back, handing it to Garcia.

"Now send in the kid," he said.

"What you going to do with her?"

"None of your business, French."

"Merry Christmas," Garcia said, tipping his hat as he smiled at the family in the next booth. He could barely contain his need to sprint from the shop. The trip back to the car seemed a lot farther than he remembered. With nervous anticipation, Garcia French slid behind the wheel, dared to glance back to the door he had exited, turned the key in the ignition, and drove quickly out the back exit. He wondered how long the boss would sit waiting.

CHAPTER 18

Officer Guiles opened the door to the captain's office, handed him the day's paper, and left. The headline read, "Where is Ruthie?" and was followed by an account of the community's watch. Although ransom was collected, the article concluded, there is no word on the child. The community is asked to be on the lookout for suspicious activity, especially in regard to children. From the television on the wall a picture of Ruthie flashed across the screen. "Elsewhere, in a case similar to the Anderson child," the reporter was saying, "the body of ten-year-old Kaci Dos was found four miles from her home in a wooded area. The child had been—"

Staring at the picture of Ruthie, the captain shot out of his chair, nearly tripping over his own feet, as he called out to Guiles. "Where's the boy?"

Surprised, Guiles replied, "Sir, you told us to turn him over to CPS when they arrived, and we did."

An amazing display of information was pelting Chester Mayfield's mind. Sadness over the death of the ten year old in another community, the sounds of Onie Smutts down the hall cursing the men, and the federal agents in the next room scrutinizing maps to the city—all were coming to a head. Adrenalin was rushing through his veins so fast he could hardly breathe.

"Get that woman from CPS on the phone, Guiles," he said when he could finally speak.

"You mean the Bennett woman?"

"Yes."

In a matter of minutes, Lori Bennett was speaking to the captain. "Mrs. Bennett, have you cleaned up that little boy yet?"

"No, sir, we didn't have clothes to fit, and I sent someone out for them. But we are ready to, and I've contacted a family that is willing to take Timmy through the holidays."

"Good. Good. Now, Mrs. Bennett, do you mind … just … putting the phone up to the child's ear that I might speak to him? I know this seems highly irregular, but we became friends in a strange sort of way. I believe the child trusts me."

Mrs. Bennett chuckled. "I can imagine that. Timmy is right here."

"Hello, this is Captain Mayfield. I met you out at the farm before I asked you if you would like to take a nice ride in the police car. Do you remember me?"

"Yes," a small tired voice answered. "But I'm not Timmy."

Captain Mayfield chuckled. "Are you Ruthie, sweetheart? If you are, I am coming right over there to pick you up and take you home to your mommy."

"Mommy calls me Sweetums, but my name is Ruthie. Ruth Elizabeth Anderson."

Captain Chester Mayfield wanted to dance around his desk; instead he said, "Ruthie, may I speak to Mrs. Bennett? Please?" He could hardly contain his joy.

"Timmy is not a boy, Mrs. Bennett. Timmy is Ruthie Anderson, the child that was kidnapped. By some miraculous twist of fate, or those praying women's faith, I strongly believe the child is our missing Ruthie." He was laughing. "I'll be right over."

He was on his way out, stopping by the door where the federal agents were on phones. When he paused to speak with them, they motioned for him to go on, mouthing they were busy. The Captain could not have been more delighted. Relief claimed every thought, where there had been fear that the little girl would not be found. Within minutes he was hurrying toward the building housing Ruthie Anderson.

"Let's keep this close to protocol, Mrs. Bennett," he said, entering the family services main office. "You will have to go with me to Mrs. Anderson's home."

Ruthie was sitting in a small child's chair, a book in one hand and an old doll scrunched up by her side. Her eyes lit up when she saw the captain. When he dropped down to a squat and opened his arms, she bounded up to slide right into his embrace. Mrs. Bennett and staff were smiling and clapping hands with joy.

"Ready, Mrs. Bennett?" The captain was beaming as he lifted Ruthie up. "You have all the important papers ready to sign, and permission for us to return Ruthie to her mother?"

"I certainly do, and I would not miss this wonderful occasion for anything."

They buckled Ruthie into the seat provided by the police department. Mrs. Bennett sat in the passenger seat up front with Captain Mayfield.

"Mrs. Bennett, I ask you to ride up here that I might ask a few questions. Since Ruthie was taken from the home by an intruder, while Mrs. Anderson was retrieving her car and the child was taken right under the nose of other adults, I wanted to make certain there were no legal entanglements for her mother."

"We have had no complaints toward Mrs. Anderson's parenting, captain. This being a kidnapping, I'm sure had you discovered the little boy at Frank Tollison's home was actually Ruthie, we would never have been called in." She sighed, shaking her head, as she glanced back at Ruthie asleep in the car seat. "It is a relief to have found this child at all. Who knows what would have happened if the lady had not gotten her car stuck in that field."

"There's more to this than we are aware of at this time," the captain replied. "Officer Guiles tells me Onie Smutts is now claiming she only took Timmy because her boyfriend planned to give the child to someone else. We cannot tell, at this point, if Onie Smutts is telling the truth, or if she has fabricated the whole thing in her mind."

"She seems very disturbed. A part of her wanted to protect the child as her son, Timmy, while another part of her seemed to be angry the child was not returning affection to her as the mother."

Lori Bennett peered at the captain.

"You understand what I mean? I couldn't read her at all. At times she appeared wistful and caring, other times filled with anger, and this little girl was truly frightened of her. You know what they say; children are the best judge of people. They know whether we are genuine or fake."

"Then it is your opinion that your people will not come after Ruthie's mother?"

"I called my superior after you said you were coming over, as I cannot be responsible for a decision concerning a child's welfare, you understand, without the input of others, and I was told in this case, we will not be interfering in Ruthie's life. But I will tell you quite honestly, our office was told to make an immediate inquiry to be 100 percent sure there are no hidden agendas in the people who surround this child daily."

"From what I observed, they are a good group of people. Their lives seemed to revolve around the child. But I will tell you, we were unable to reach the father, and that concerns me greatly. No disrespect intended," the captain said. "But it would not be the first time a parent kidnapped his own child. The only difference here is a parent normally would not ask for ransom." A laughing boisterous Captain Mayfield said, as the Anderson home came into view. "I cannot tell you how happy I am to bring this child home." He parked on the street, climbing out to open the back door, unbuckle, and collect Ruthie in his arms. "I radioed ahead to Miller that we would arrive within minutes." He had no more finished the sentence than Ruthie's mother came bounding down the steps from where she had been waiting on the porch.

"Ruthie," she was calling her child as she ran. "Ruthie. Ruthie."

Ruthie stirred, peering up at the captain. "Is that Momma?"

"You bet your boots," he grinned, handing her over to Ellen Anderson.

"Sweetums. Sweetums." Tears were streaming down Ellen's face as she kissed Ruthie over and over and again. "My baby," she sighed, settling her face into Ruthie's neck. "Where have you been, Sweetums? I missed you."

"I've been too many places," Ruthie replied crossly. "I don't ever want to go again."

Bitty stood to one side. "Go on," Harriet prodded. "You know Ruthie wants you."

"I can't, Harriet." She pulled the hem of the apron she was wearing up to wipe away the tears.

"Ruthie's grandparents deserve a chance to get to know her."

"And that's not all, is it?" Harriet's tone had gentled. "You have thought all along Ellen might harbor thoughts of who was to blame. And no one was. Ellen knew you and Anne were here, and you knew she was going for her car. It was a stranger invaded the house, Bitty. Evil was done, unbeknownst to any of you, and now that Ruthie has been found, just thank God no one was hurt when that person violated your space and took what was not theirs. I tell you who is to blame. The person behind the kidnapping."

"I have such fear there will be repercussion to the whole thing," Bitty whispered. "And Anne is another problem. She won't have anyone to go home to when she leaves the hospital." Bitty sighed. "Maybe you and I can go see her now that Ellen's parents will be here for her and Ruthie."

"What are you saying, Bitty?" Harriet frowned. "Are you leaving, Ellen?"

"For a time, I believe so. They need to reunite and become acquainted again." Bitty turned toward the kitchen. "I changed the sheets on the bed in the attic, and everything has been washed up and is drying right now. Much as I'll miss being here, I think Anne needs us now … anyway me. And that's what I intend to do."

"Well, of course I'll help with Anne. But that means you will have to pick me up. I don't have a car." Harriet smiled. "That would mean you could look in on Ruthie and Ellen every day, too."

Bitty was busy at the kitchen sink, listening to Harriet, when she felt a tug at her apron strings and the warmth of a small body hurtling itself at her. "Bitty. Bitty." Ruthie wrapped her arms around Bitty, pressing her face into the small of Bitty's back. "You didn't see me, did you, Bitty? You didn't know I'm here."

"Lands of mercy. Is that you, Ruthie?" Bitty turned, stooping, her eyes on a level with Ruthie. "Why, it *is* you. I thought you were hiding in the attic. I have looked everywhere for you." For a moment, Bitty's heart did a flip-flop in her chest. Ruthie, though appearing none the worse for the wear, looked a bit tattered in boy clothes and pale faced, but weren't they all? It was Ruthie's hair, her beautiful Shirley Temple hair, chopped off in a helter-skelter way. "Lands, child, you look like one of those orphans we saw in that book. Where was that?" Bitty hugged Ruthie, laughing with love. "I missed you so much I cried. Can you believe that?"

"No. You don't cry." Ruthie protested, climbing on Bitty's lap as she sat on the kitchen chair. Taking Bitty's face between her hands, Ruthie's eyes became warm liquid pools of trust as she gently rubbed her friend's face. "I didn't like that woman, Bitty. She called me Timmy and told me to call her Momma. I didn't like her."

"That's the way it is sometime, Ruthie. We try, but we don't always like everyone."

Pointing toward the police captain, Ruthie said, "He said I was sodden. You know what that means, Bitty? My clothes were wet because she pulled me like we pull our wagon, 'cept I don't have wheels and sometimes it hurt." Bitty's arms tightened around Ruthie. "You ever been sodden, Bitty?" Tears in her eyes, Bitty shook her head. "See. We learned something, Bitty. Sodden means wet."

As Ruthie settled more into her lap, Bitty wondered what else Ruthie learned, and thought time would tell, and she would be around to help her with it when the time come for Ellen's parents to return to their home. For now, as Ruthie yawned, Bitty said, "You know, Ruthie, your grandparents might want to sleep upstairs in my bed. I am wondering if you could show them where things are, and I'll go on home and maybe I will go see Anne on the way. What do you think?"

"Why do you need to see Anne?" Ruthie yawned. "I need you to see me, Bitty."

"Well, you are going to be awfully busy with your grandparents, and Mommy will want to spend time alone with you. How about when they have to go home, I come back and we will learn something new again? Every day?"

"Bitty, can the policeman come see if you are all right? He said he would see me every day for a while, because he likes me. I like him too. Can he, Bitty?"

Laughing, Bitty planted a kiss on top of Ruthie's chopped off hair. "I guess so." She stood Ruthie on the floor. "Now scoot. Go see Mommy. She is waiting for you."

As they talked, Ellen and her new friend, Daniel, watched Ruthie returning to her mother. Tears filled Bitty's eyes once more. How sweet the hurt of being loved. *When you love someone*, she thought, *there's always the fear of loss*, and they had almost lost Ruthie.

Looking up, Bitty sent a message to Larry. "Well, husband, I guess I'm learning the hard way. But I do believe I'm learning to trust the Lord again, and He must have heard our prayers. How else would we have Ruthie back?" She almost could hear Larry laughing.

Taking Ellen's mother aside, Bitty explained about Anne's wreck. There were so many things to tell the woman, Bitty feared she would feel swamped. "I'll be in and out," she promised. "Ruthie knows where everything is, and how it all works."

"We will do our best, Bitty." Ellen's mother hugged her as though they were old friends. "I can see how much they both love you," she said. "And we will too."

On her way out, the captain stepped over to open and close the door, taking her suitcase without asking, just relieving the load. "I'll be needing your address," he said, a solemn expression on his face. Bitty peered up, wondering if indeed the problems she had imagined were coming to bear. "It's a matter of police business," he added. They walked on a few steps to Bitty's car. "Ruthie insisted I have to check on you daily, Mrs. Shaw."

Frustrated, Bitty opened her mouth to speak. "I don't think that's appropriate, Captain Mayfield. You best be going home to check on your wife. Any man that stays away from home and family as many hours as you have this weekend shouldn't give it another thought."

Matter of factly, Bitty opened the car door while he placed the suitcase in the back seat, turned the key in the ignition, and as the engine fired, finished her sentence. "Go home, Captain Mayfield. I don't need you checking on me."

"There's just one problem, ma'am. My wife died about five years ago, and my family lives in another state." Laying his hands on the roof of the car he leaned in, his face on a closer level with hers. "It's a pretty lonely life, ma'am. What I've seen this weekend reminded me how close-knit and loving friends and family can be. It brought to my mind what I miss the most." Backing away, he gave a salute, "It's been a pleasure to meet you, Mrs. Shaw, even under these stressful circumstances." He paused." I'm certainly glad we found little Ruthie. Folks in a nearby town were not so fortunate. We have much to be thankful for."

Driving away, Bitty was aware the police captain stood watching until she was out of sight. Now why would he do that? It was perplexing, and she had no time to figure it out. She was heading to the hospital to check on Anne's progress. Tomorrow she would return to see how Ellen and Ruthie were faring, and then she and Harriet would see about Anne again. She had to put the captain out of her mind. He was a very disturbing man when one thought about it. He was more than a foot taller than Bitty's small frame, and then some. At times, she had caught his eyes on her, which had only increased the pain she felt in her heart with Ruthie missing. Wasn't she the one watched over the child each day? Though he asked, there seemed to be some unspoken questions, and she wondered how he could possibly think she might be part of the kidnapping. Then, she had reasoned, any one of them was suspect. Sensing the unasked questions had almost hardened her heart against the man. But she had seen his gentleness and compassion in handling Ellen throughout the ordeal. And he was bursting with happiness in bringing Ruthie home. It was obvious Ruthie had touched his heart, and the child trusts him. Still, in her heart, Bitty felt the repercussions she had feared had to do with Captain Mayfield. Yes, he was a perplexing man, and she didn't know why.

Returning to the house, Chester glanced around the room, his eyes lingering on the mother holding her child and the content of the man sitting next to them taking it all in. The grandparents were absent, he supposed investigating the room upstairs he had overheard Bitty speaking about with Ruthie. It was obvious, as caretaker of the child, Bitty's need was to rush forward and hug the little girl, but she held back for the sake of the grandparents. Ruthie's eyes had sought first her mother and then Bitty. It must have seemed an eternity until she found herself sitting on either of their laps.

Motioning to Daniel Gates, the captain asked him to step outside.

"My job's done here," he said, extending his hand. "If there are any questions, please tell Mrs. Anderson to call me." He drew a card from behind the cell phone in his shirt pocket. "This is my number, and I'm available at any time."

"I don't think Ellen is going to let you get away with just a card," Daniel grinned as Ellen came forward.

"I know you are tired, Captain Mayfield, and I hope you can rest now that Ruthie is home safely. May I hug you, and thank you for being here with us? Your presence was a calming effect in the worst hours." She put her arms around the man. "Thank you, from the bottom of my heart."

Daniel followed the captain to the car. "I want to extend my gratitude, too, sir."

"Take care of them, young man. You have quite an impressive young woman there." He laid a second card in Daniel's hand. "As you know, the money was marked."

"I gathered as much."

"We did not ask for the numbers to be in sequence. However, the untrained eye would be unable to read the identifying mark. If our person starts spending money in another state, we've got him." The captain's eyes narrowed in speculation, "It is my opinion that this person pushed through with more bluff than experience." Scrubbing a foot against the loose pebbles on the drive, he continued. "Mind you now, I'm not saying a first-time offender would not hurt a child or anyone who gets in his way, because he would to protect himself, but this rings of someone new at the game. Someone that forgot to read the rules on punishment in accordance with kidnapping. Punishment by death. He blundered through and got lucky. I think we are going to hear from him pretty soon."

"So you don't think it was the lady, Onie Smutts?"

"No, sir, I don't. That one will plead not guilty by some far out reason. She will be punished for her part in it, and if there's a boyfriend, as she says, it's possible he will receive the highest punishment, unless he is an accomplice and willing to give up whoever set the whole miserable mess in motion." He sighed. "They will all go to prison, in my opinion. We'll see."

CHAPTER 19

The boss, as he had come to call himself, slung a bag containing a gift wrapped package in the back seat of his Altima Nissan. He had driven across town, from the hotel where he stayed, to dispose of the fake hairpiece and mustache, the tortoise-shelled glasses, and the can of disinfectant that made him cough and hack like an emphysema patient.

A niggle of concern sliced with guilt crept into his conscience now and then, but since all had ended well, he would put that aside and concentrate on getting home. Nila would be waiting to hear how the business trip had gone. "Lucrative," he would say. "I believe we can begin anew." The miles flew behind him, Nashville, Knoxville, almost halfway. Flipping the radio station to station, he settled on the news.

"The child kidnapped in Missouri has been found. Although ransom was paid, the person responsible for taking little Ruthie Anderson escaped. Even now, the people of the community have returned. Let us listen as well-wishers and the choir from Christ Church are now rejoicing with song."

"So they rejoice. Salt of the earth people." He pressed the knob and the radio was silenced. From the slideshow of his mind, he could see the mother, the child, and the people singing. Angst spread, searing across his heart, running pell-mell through his veins, vicious, inflictive, and cruel, claiming its hold as the angels of good and bad did battle.

CHAPTER 20

THE HOUSE WAS QUIET AS the clock in the hall struck, the gong melodiously sounding nine times. Ruthie had been scrubbed and put to bed. The grandparents were climbing the stairs for a second time, happily weary to have a bed with clean sheets on which to lay their heads. Inside the privacy of the room, they embraced. No words were necessary. Downstairs, both daughter and grandchild were fine.

"Long day," Daniel said to Ellen. "I think you have had enough traumas to last a life time."

"I can't thank you enough," she replied.

"Well, actually, you can." He grinned. "Don't think I'm leaving without staking my claim." He traced a heart on the top of her hand. "We've been through the best and the worst of times today. It made an impression on me and I hope on you."

She sighed, leaning into the curve of his arm. "I can't imagine why this feels so natural. It is as though I've waited for this all my life." Hesitant to continue, she studied their entwined hands. "I don't mean to give you the wrong impression" she sighed. "You know my past. You know where I'm headed. But it is so good to … have someone," she struggled. "A friend."

"I think we have crossed that line, Ellen. This whole situation has given us opportunity to see in each other what it could have taken years to see."

Blushing and embarrassed, Ellen sought the right words. If she read too much into the moment, Daniel might think she expected more than he was willing to give, if she faltered. "You can say that," she said finally. "I can't. You have given your all while I have so little to give."

"Ellen. Except for the fact that I know you need more time, I would ask you today, right now, to marry me, to be my wife." He slid to the floor, on one knee. "We have both been hurt. But your pain had to be much worse than mine."

Leaning in, he kissed Ellen, not the usual kiss on the hair, but a lingering, questioning kiss that stirred the depth of their emotions, burning a need into their hearts. With Ruthie's return, they could turn their minds toward good things to come, moments and years of contentment that would fuel the desire to build something that would last through eternity.

"Remember, you mentioned a friend?" His fingers straightened a loose strand of hair as he peered into her face and then laid one finger beneath her chin, an endearment she had come to expect. "A good marriage should start with friendship. But it wasn't friendship I saw in you that first day I met you at Schumacher's. I fell hard that day, Ellen Anderson, and I knew from that minute on, I intend to do everything within my power to make you my wife."

Tears streamed silently down her face, and as he wiped them away, Ellen felt hope. "I never really thought I'd trust a man again," she whispered. "But you speak to my heart and my soul cries out."

Daniel rose to his feet. "I thought you would never tell me how you really feel. My poor old injured football knee was screaming. But I'd have stayed there till dawn, if that's what it takes." He grinned, pulling her up. "Was that a *yes*, to marrying me?"

"First things first—don't you think you should get to know my daughter?"

"She is a little charmer. I'm smitten already," he admitted.

"So …?"

She looped her arms around his neck; although her eyebrows were raised, there was a smile on her face. She laid one finger gently against his lips.

"All right, I'll take it slow, and I will enjoy every minute of this courtship, but you have already been warned. I intend to make you my wife." With that said, he lifted her off her feet and swung her around joyously. For the first time in days, Ellen laughed, and it felt good.

"I love you," Daniel said as his lips claimed hers.

Blushing, Ellen threw all caution to the wind and replied. "I love you too."

The End

Made in the USA
Middletown, DE
23 October 2014